The Author

HUBERT AQUIN was born in Montreal, Quebec, in 1929. After receiving his licentiate in philosophy from the University of Montreal, he spent three years at the Institute of Political Studies in Paris, then returned to the University of Montreal, where he studied for one year at the Institute of History.

Aquin worked as a radio and television producer with the Canadian Broadcasting Corporation's Public Affairs division in Montreal and won many awards for his work as a director with the National Film Board.

One of Quebec's prominent essayists, he turned to fiction in the 1960s. *Next Episode* (1965), Aquin's first novel, is the searing first-person account of terrorism about to be perpetrated by the novel's young narrator.

Hubert Aquin died in Montreal, Quebec, in 1977.

THE NEW CANADIAN LIBRARY

General Editor: David Staines

Hubert Aquin

NEXT EPISODE

Translated by Sheila Fischman

With an Afterword by Jean-Louis Major

This translation is dedicated to the memory of my friend Alan Brown, the distinguished translator who introduced me to Hubert Aquin and took me into his world.

Prochain Épisode
Original edition published by Le Cercle du Livre de France
Copyright © 1965 by Hubert Aquin
Next Episode
Translated from the French by Sheila Fischman
Copyright © 2001 by the Estate of Hubert Aquin
Afterword copyright © by Jean-Louis Major

New Canadian Library edition 2001

National Library of Canada Cataloguing in Publication

Aquin, Hubert, 1929-1977
[Prochain épisode. English]
Next episode

(New Canadian library)
Translation of: Prochain épisode.
Previously published under title: Prochain episode.
Includes bibliographical references.
ISBN 0-7710-3471-7

I. Fischman, Sheila.   II. Title   III. Title: Prochain episode.
IV. Title: Prochain épisode. English.   V. Series.

PS8501.P85P713 2001   C843'.54   C00-933203-0
PQ3919.2.A66P713 2001

We acknowledge the financial support of the Government of Canada through the Book Publishing Industry Development Program and that of the Government of Ontario through the Ontario Media Development Corporation's Ontario Book Initiative. We further acknowledge the support of the Canada Council for the Arts and the Ontario Arts Council for our publishing program.

Typesetting by M&S, Toronto
Printed and bound in Canada

McClelland & Stewart Ltd.
The Canadian Publishers
481 University Avenue
Toronto, Ontario
M5G 2E9
www.mcclelland.com/NCL

3 4 5   07 06 05 04 03

So you're in the Alps! Are they not beautiful? There is nothing else in the world.

– Alfred de Musset[1]

[1] *Correspondence of G. Sand and Alfred de Musset* (Brussels: E. Deman, 1904), p. 40.

CUBA IS SINKING in flames in the middle of Lac Léman while I descend to the bottom of things. Packed inside my sentences, I glide, a ghost, into the river's neurotic waters, discovering as I drift the underside of surfaces and the inverted image of the Alps. Between the anniversary of the Cuban revolution and the date of my trial, I have time enough to ramble on in peace, to open my unpublished book with great care, and to cover this paper with the key-words that won't set me free. I'm writing on a card table next to a window looking out on grounds enclosed by a sharp iron fence that marks the boundary between what's unpredictable and what is locked up. I won't get out before the day of reckoning. That's written in several carbon copies as decreed, following valid laws and an unassailable royal judge. There are no distractions then, nothing to replace the clockwork of my obsession or make me deviate from the written record of my journey. Basically, only one thing really concerns me and it's this: how should I set about writing a spy novel? My wish is complicated by the fact that I long to do something original in a genre that has so many unwritten rules and laws. Fortunately, though, a certain laziness leads me to give up any idea about breathing new life into the tradition before I even get started. I may as well admit it – making myself comfortable in a literary form that's already so well defined makes me feel very secure. And so without hesitation I decide to integrate my work within the main lines of the traditional spy novel. And since I want to set it in Lausanne, that's taken care of. As quickly as I can, I eliminate any behaviour that would give my secret agent too much merit: he's neither a Sphinx nor a highly perceptive Tarzan, neither God nor the Holy Ghost; he mustn't be so logical that the plot need not be or, on the other hand, so lucid that I can complicate everything else and cook up some story that makes no sense, that when all's said and done would only be understood by some bungling oaf with a gun who doesn't share his thoughts with anyone. And if I were to introduce a Wolof Secret Agent . . . Everybody knows that Wolofs aren't legion in French-speaking Switzerland and that they're under-represented in the secret service. I know, I'm overdoing it, falling into the trap of the Afro-Asian bloc, giving in to the African and Madagascar Union lobby. But let me tell you something: if Hamidou Diop suits me, I can simply make him a secret agent in Lausanne on a counter-espionage mission, for no other reason than to get him out of Geneva where the air is less salubrious. Now I can reserve a suite at the Lausanne Palace for Hamidou, provide him with traveller's cheques from the Banque Cantonale Vaudoise, and appoint him a Special Envoy (a phony one) from the Republic of Senegal to some big Swiss companies that want to invest in desert real estate. Once Hamidou is protected by his fake identity and settled in at the Lausanne Palace, I can bring CIA and MI5 agents into the picture. And that's that. In return for adding a few alluring lady spies and the algebraic treatment of the plot, I have my deal. Hamidou is getting impatient, I sense that he's about to do something crazy: in fact, I suspect it's already begun. My future novel is already in orbit, so far out that I can't bring it back. I'm frozen, I've just been dumped here inside my alphabet, I'm shackled to it and asking myself some questions. To write the kind of spy novel we read would be dishonest: in fact, it would be impossible. Writing a story is no small matter, unless it becomes the daily and detailed punctuation of my endless stillness and my slow fall into this liquid pit. The enemy will be lying in wait for me unless I can make life absolutely impossible for my character. To populate my own empty space I intend to pile up corpses along my character's way, multiply attempts on his life, drive him crazy with anonymous calls and knives planted in his bedroom door; I'll kill everyone he's spoken to, even the courteous hotel cashier. I'll put Hamidou through the mill or I won't have the courage to live. I'll plant bombs in his entourage and to complicate matters conclusively I'll set the Chinese onto him, a number of them and all the same: there will be Chinese on the streets of Lausanne, hordes of smiling Chinese who'll look Hamidou in the eye. Taking a Stelazine distracted me briefly from poor Hamidou's career. Fifteen minutes from now they'll bring me a cold meal, and other interruptions will go on till bedtime, as I draw up the outline of a novel without continuity, lay down the unknowns of a fictitious equation, and in the end imagine some total nonsense for as long as this disorganized siege gives me a bulwark against sadness and the criminal waves that crash into me, roaring and chanting the name of the woman I love.

Late one winter afternoon we drove through the country-side around Acton Vale. Patches of snow on the hillsides reminded us of the dazzling snow that had enfolded our first embrace in the nondescript apartment on Côte-des-Neiges. On that lonely road which goes from Saint-Liboire to Upton and then to Acton Vale, from Acton Vale to Durham-sud, from Durham-sud to Melbourne, Richmond, Danville, Chénier, formerly known as Tingwick, we talked to each other, my love. For the first time we mingled our two lives in a river of inspiration that still flows in me this afternoon between the shattered shores of Lac Léman. It's in the area of this invisible lake that I'll set my story, it's into the very waters of the extended Rhône that I plunge, tirelessly seeking my own cadaver. The quiet road from Acton Vale to Durham-sud is the end of the world. Thrown off track, I descend into myself but I can't find my way. Imprisoned in a clinical submarine, I'm engulfed by a deathly uncertainty. The only thing that's certain now is your secret name, your warm, wet mouth, your amazing body I reinvent again and again with less precision and more passion. I count the days I have to live without you and my chances of finding you again after I've wasted all that time: how can I avoid doubt? How can I avoid choosing suicide over this atrocious erosion? Everything from the past is crumbling. I lose all notion of the time of passion, I even lose any awareness of my slow escape, for I have no point of reference to help me measure my speed. Nothing is hardening outside my window: characters and memories are liquefied in the pointless splendour of the alpine lake where I try to find my words. I've already spent twenty-two days away from your resplendent body. I have sixty more days of underwater residence before I resume our interrupted embrace or set out again on the road to prison. For now, I'm at a table at the bottom of Lac Léman, plunged into its fluid sphere of influence which supplants my subconscious, joining my own depression to the languid depression of the Cimbrian Rhône, my imprisonment to the widening of its shores. I'm attending my own resolution. I inspect the ripples, keep an eye on everything that happens here; I listen at the doors of the Lausanne Palace and I'm wary of the Alps. In Vevey the other night, I stopped for a beer at the Café Vaudois. As I was skimming through the paper, I saw a brief item I tore out when no one was looking. It read: "Tuesday, August 1, the distinguished professor H. de Heutz of the University of Basel will speak on 'Caesar and the Helvetians,' under the auspices of the Société d'Histoire de la Suisse romande, 7 rue Jacques-Dalcroze, Geneva. Shortly before the vernal equinox in the year 58, the Helvetians had grouped north of Lac Léman to prepare for a mass exodus towards transalpine Gaul. This concentration, carried out a few miles from Genaba (now Geneva), intending to cross the Rhône over that city's bridge, thereby encroaching on the integrity of transalpine Gaul, determined Caesar's behaviour. The war between Caesar and the courageous Helvetians will be the subject of the presentation by the eminent Professor H. de Heutz." Mystified by this speech and by the subtle correlation I've detected between that chapter of Swiss history and certain features of my own story, I stuffed the notice in my wallet and promised myself that I'd go to Geneva on August 1 and kill some time by killing several thousand Helvetians with beacons just to keep in practice.

Daylight is fading. The tall trees that line the Institute grounds are bombarded by light. Never have they appeared so cruel to me and never have I felt so much like a prisoner. Troubled, too, by what I'm writing, I'm very weary and tempted to give in to inertia the way one gives in to a fascination. Why should I go on writing and what shall I say? Why draw curves on paper when I long to go out, to stroll, to run towards the woman I love, to abolish myself in her and sweep her away with me into my resurrection and towards death? No, I no longer know why I'm writing this puzzle while I suffer and the hydrous vise is tightening over my temples till it crushes my few remaining memories. Something inside me is threatening to explode. There are more and more cracking sounds, foreshadowing a seismic event that my scattered activities can no longer keep at bay. Two or three censored novels can't distract me from the free world I see out my window, from which I'm excluded. Volume IX of the complete works of Balzac is particularly discouraging. "In Paris under the Empire thirteen men met, all struck by the same sentiment, all energetic enough to follow the same line of thinking, political enough to conceal the sacred bonds that united them . . ." I stop here. The opening sentence of the *Story of the Thirteen* slays me; that dazzling beginning makes me want to end my own cumulative prose, just as it reminds me of the sacred bonds, now broken by isolation, that once joined me to my revolutionary brothers. I have nothing to gain from going on writing. But I go on anyway, though I'm writing at a loss. No, that's a lie: for the past few minutes I've known perfectly well that I will gain something from this game, I'll gain time: an interval I cover with erasures and phonemes, fill with syllables and howls, cram with all my acknowledged atoms, multiples of a totality they'll never equal. I compose in highly automatic writing and while I'm spelling myself, I avoid homicidal lucidity. I dazzle myself with words. And I drift complacently because this procedure lets me gain in minutes what I lose proportionately in despair. I stuff the page with mental mincemeat, I cram it to the bursting point with syntax, I pound at the naked paper, I can barely keep from writing with both hands at once, so I'll think less. And suddenly I land on my feet, safe and sound but drained, tired as an invalid after the crisis. Now that the deed is done and Balzac eliminated, the pain of vainly desiring the woman I love avoided, now that I've chopped my fury into devalued notions, I feel rested and I can look at the submerged landscape, I can count the trees I no longer see, recollect the names of the streets in Lausanne. I can easily recall the smell of fresh paint in my cell at the Montreal Prison and the stench of the Municipal Police cubicles. Now that I'm feeling free and easy, I let incoherence take hold of me again; I give in to that improvised stream, renouncing more from laziness than principle the premeditated plotting of a genuine novel. Real novels I leave to the real novelists. As for me, I flatly refuse to bring algebra into my invention. Condemned to a certain ontological incoherence, I take my stand. I'm even turning it into a system with an immediate application that I decree. Infinite I shall be, in my own way and in the literal sense. I won't leave a system I create for the sole purpose of never leaving it. As a matter of fact I'm not leaving anything, not even here. I'm caught, compressed inside a hermetically sealed glass booth. From my prison window I can see a red van – how suspicious! – that reminds me of another red van that was parked on Pine Avenue one morning outside the *porte-cochère* of the Mount Royal Fusiliers. But now the red stain is moving away and disappearing into the darkness, depriving me of a bracing memory. Bye bye Mount Royal Fusiliers. Farewell to arms! That unexpected play on words gets me down: I feel like dissolving into tears, I'm not sure why. All those weapons stolen from the enemy, hidden and then discovered in sorrow one by one, all those weapons! And I who am disarmed here for having held a weapon, disarmed as well before the idling sun as it quietly sets behind Île Jésus! If I give in to the twilight again, I won't be able to hold my position for very long or to manoeuvre serenely in the stagnant waters of fiction. If I look at the vanished sun again, I won't have the strength to bear the time I saw passing between you and me, between our two bodies stretched out on the calendar of spring and summer, then suddenly broken at the beginning of Cancer. I must close my eyes, tighten my grip on the pen, not give in to the pain, not believe in miracles or in the litanies I utter every night beneath the sheet, not invoke your name, my love. I mustn't speak it aloud, write it on this paper, sing it, cry it. I must silence it and let my heart break.

I'm breathing through lungs of steel. What comes to me from outside is filtered, drained of oxygen and nothingness, making me more frail. I'm subjected to a psychiatric evaluation before being sent to trial. But I know that this very expertise contains an unspoken assumption that confers legitimacy on the system I'm fighting and a pathological connotation on my own undertaking. Psychiatry is the science of individual imbalance enclosed within a flawless society. It enhances the standing of conformists and the well-integrated, not those who refuse; it glorifies all forms of civil obedience and acceptance. It's not just solitude I'm battling here, but the clinical imprisonment that casts doubt on my effectiveness as a revolutionary.

I might as well reread Balzac! I want to identify with Ferragus, to live magically the story of a man condemned by society, yet capable on his own of standing up to the police stranglehold and avoiding capture by mimicking it, both its dual nature and its constant shifting and moving. I've dreamed about that, too, about fleeing to a different apartment every day, dressing in my hosts' clothes, concealing my escapes in a ritual of parades and productions. Because I draped myself unwittingly in Ferragus's spotted garments, today I'm in a clinic under surveillance after an inglorious stay in the Montreal Prison. It all seems to me like a tremendous act of cheating, including my pain when I confess it. The deeper I sink into disenchantment, the more I discover the arid soil where for years I thought I saw a mythical vegetation spring up, a true hallucinatory debauchery, a flowering of false-hood and style to mask a plain that had been close-cropped, shattered, burned by the sun of lucidity and boredom: myself! Now the truth won't let me seed it with a forest of calyxes. My own face, unveiled once and for all, terrifies me. Having come here as a prisoner, I feel myself sicken from day to day. Nothing feeds my soul any more: no starry night transmutes my desert into sheets of shadow and mystery. Nothing offers me distraction or some substitute euphoria. Everything abandons me at the speed of light, all the membranes break, allowing the precious blood to seep away.

BETWEEN JULY 26, 1960 and August 4, 1792, halfway between two liberations, while I worm my way, coated in a light alloy, into a novel being written in Lausanne, I'm anxiously looking for a man who left the Lausanne Palace after shaking hands with Hamidou Diop. I slipped into the hotel lobby without attracting Hamidou's attention. Executing a *paso doble*, I was outside the hotel a fraction of a second later, in time to see a 300SL drive off towards Place Saint-François. Something told me that this fleeting silhouette didn't pop out of the Senegalese Sahel and that Hamidou is playing a double game. In any case, it's pointless to ask him to identify the man he was speaking to, or tell him about my own rash suspicions. The handsome African is more cunning than a Chinese. With his unbridled loquacity and his athletic negritude, he masks all too successfully both his wiles and his awe-inspiring intelligence.

During these reflections on my hero's subtle duplicity, I walked slowly up the rue de Bourg and went inside the movie theatre on Place Benjamin Constant to see *Black Orpheus* again. Listening to ".Felicidade," I started to cry. I don't know why that song of happiness spells melancholy to me or why that fragile joy was translated for me into lugubrious chords. So nothing can stop me from calling to my black Eurydice, from searching for her in the never-ending night, shadow among the shadows of a dark carnival, a night darker than a night of saturnalia, a night sweeter than the one we spent together somewhere in her native tropics one June 24. Eurydice, I am descending. I'm here, at last. By writing to you I shall touch you, black shadow, black magic, love. The Benjamin Constant theatre is a free fall for me. This very evening, a few miles from the Hôtel de la Paix, headquarters of the FLN, a few steps from the Montreal Prison, dark headquarters of the FLQ, no sooner do I brush against your blazing body than it's lost to me; I piece you together again but words fail me. The historic night seems to be secreting the India ink in which I can make out too many fleeting forms that resemble you but aren't you. At the end of my liquid decadence, I'll touch the low land, our bed of caresses and convulsions. My love . . . I feel giddy. In fact I'm afraid of every silhouette, of my neighbours in the theatre, of the stranger who conceals Eurydice's mulatto profile from me, of the people waiting on the sidewalk when I leave the theatre.

I hurried through this dense crowd and crossed Place Benjamin Constant. And as I walked past the illuminated front of the Hôtel de la Paix, I looked in the other direction at the jagged profile of the Savoy Alps and the mottled expanse of the lake. Eleven-fifteen. I'd wasted my day. Now I had nothing to do, no one to meet, no hope of finding the man Hamidou had shaken hands with in the lobby of the Lausanne Palace. Nonchalantly, I went back to the hotel. I was given the key to my room and a sealed blue paper. I tore it open quickly, and understanding nothing of what was written on it, I stuffed it into my pocket so I wouldn't attract the elevator boy's attention. As soon as I was in my room I lay down on the bed and reread the formless jumble of capital letters with no spaces: CINBEUPERFLEUDIARUNCOBESCUBEREBES-CUAZURANOCTIVAGUS. This one-word cryptogram had me perplexed for a few minutes; then I decided to perform an alphabetical statistical analysis, which gave me: E 7 times; U 7; R 5; B, A, and C 4 times; S 3; I 3; O 2; G 2; P, F, L, V, and Z one time only. The blatant predominance of the letter U was mystifying. I know of no language in which that vowel is so predominant. Not even in Portuguese and Romanian, though they're rife with U's, does that letter so outweigh the other vowels.

The cryptogram from the Hôtel de la Paix still fascinates me, not only because of its mysterious origin (which has nothing to do with the Bureau, whose figures and even their variants I know by heart), but also because of why the message was sent. As I stumbled over this equation with its multiple unknowns I must solve before I go any further in my story, I have the feeling I'm facing the most impenetrable mystery of all. The more I circle it and target it, the further it moves beyond my grasp, multiplying my own riddle tenfold even as I step up my efforts to grasp it. I simply don't seem able to decipher the code, and since I can't translate it into my language, I write it down in the insane hope that by paraphrasing the nameless, I'll finally give it a name. Yet even though I cover this hieroglyph with words, it gets away from me and I'm left behind on the other shore, surrounded by vagueness and hope. Crowded inside my closed sphere, I descend, compressed, to the bottom of Lac Léman, and I can't step outside the flowing themes that constitute the thread of the plot. I've closed myself inside a constellate system that has imprisoned me in strictly literary terms, so much so that this stylistic sequestration seems to confirm the validity of the symbol I've used from the outset: diving. Encased in my funerary barque and my repertoire of images, I have only to continue drowning through words. Descending is my future, diving my sole activity and my profession. I drown. I become Ophelia in the Rhône. My long manuscript tresses mingle with water plants and invariable adverbs while I glide, variable, between the two long jagged shores of the cisalpine river. And so duly coffered inside my metallic concept, certain that I won't get out but uncertain as to whether I'll live for a long time, I have just one thing to do: open my eyes, look at this flooded world, pursue the man I'm looking for and kill him.

Kill! What a splendid law, one it's sometimes good to comply with. For months now I've been preparing myself inwardly for killing in cold blood and with maximum precision. On that rainy Sunday morning I was secretly preparing to strike. My heart was beating steadily, my mind was clear, agile, precise as a weapon has to be. The months and months that had gone before had genuinely transformed me. And it was with an acute sense of the gravity of my effort and with reflexes perfectly trained that I was inaugurating this black wedding day. Suddenly, around half-past ten, the break occurred. Arrest, handcuffs, interrogation, disarmament. An unqualified disaster, this trite accident that earned me nothing but a stay in jail is an anti-dialectical event and the flagrant contradiction of the undeclared plan I was going to carry out, weapon in hand, in the purifying euphoria of fanaticism. Killing confers a style on one's existence. And the prospect of it, when shamefully introduced into everyday life, injects it with the energy it needs to avoid feeble crawling and endless boredom. After my trial and my liberation I can't imagine my life outside the homicide axis. Already I'm bursting with impatience at the thought of the multiple attack, a pure and shattering act that will restore my appetite for life and establish me as a terrorist in the strictest privacy. And that violence will bring order back to my life, because it seems to me that, for thirty-four years now, I've only lived the way that grass lives. If I were to make a quick tally of kisses given, of my powerful emotions, of my nights of wonder, of my luminous days, of the privileged hours and the great discoveries I have yet to make; and if I were to add up over an infinity of perforated postcards the cities I've passed through, the hotels where I've had a good meal or a night of love, the number of my friends and of the women I've betrayed, to what sombre inventory would these irregular operations lead me? The sine curve of real-life experience doesn't translate the ancient hope. I've perverted my life line repeatedly and obtained less happiness through an accumulation of indignities, which has led me to give back less than nothing of it. Before this inborn statistic that suddenly and wearily haunts me, I can imagine nothing better than to continue writing on this sheet of paper and to plunge hopelessly into the ghostly lake that's flooding into me. To descend word by word into my memory pit, to invent other companions who already perturb me, leading me into a knot of wrong tracks and, finally, to go into exile once and for all outside my botched country.

Between a certain July 26 and the Amazonian night of August 4, somewhere between the Montreal Prison and my point of fall, I decline silently, under house arrest and beneath the wing of Viennese psychiatry; my morale is low and I concede the obvious: that this breakdown is my way of existing. For years I've lived flattened with fury. I've accustomed my friends to an intolerable voltage, to a waste of sparks and short circuits. To spit fire, to cheat death, to be resurrected a hundred times, to run a mile in less than four minutes, to introduce a flame-thrower into the dialectic and suicidal behaviour into politics – that's how I've established my style. I have struck my currency amid the image of a flabby *übermensch*. A pirate set free in a misty pond, covered by a Colt 38 and injected with intoxicating syringes, I'm a prisoner, a terrorist, an anarchist, and an undeniably washed-up revolutionary! With my gun at my hip, always ready for a lightning shot at ghosts, never pulling my punches and with a heavy heart, I'm the hero, the former addict! National leader of an unknown people! I am the fragmented symbol of Quebec's revolution, its fractured reflection and its suicidal incarnation. Since the age of fifteen I've always wanted a fine suicide: under the snow-covered ice of Lac du Diable, in the northern waters of the St. Lawrence estuary, in a room at the Windsor Hotel with a woman I loved, in the car that was crushed last winter, in the little bottle of Beta-Chlor 500 mg, in the bed of the Totem, in the ravines of the Grande-Casse and the Tower of Aï, in my cell number CG19, in the words I learned at school, in my throat choked with emotion, in my ungrasped jugular gushing blood! To commit suicide everywhere, with no respite – that is my mission. Within myself, explosive and depressed, an entire nation grovels historically and recounts its lost childhood in bursts of stammered words and scriptural raving, and then, under the dark shock of lucidity, suddenly begins to weep at the enormity of the disaster, at the nearly sublime scope of its failure. There comes a time, after two centuries of conquest and thirty-four years of confusional sorrow, when one no longer has the strength to go beyond the appalling vision. Shut away inside the Institute walls and outfitted with the file of a terrorist who suffers ghostly maniacal phases, I give in to the vertiginous act of writing my memoirs and I start writing up the precise and meticulous proceedings of an unending suicide. There comes a time when fatigue erodes even unassailable plans and the novel one has begun unsystematically to write is diluted in equanitrate. The wages of the broken warrior are depression. The wages of our national depression are my own failure; it's my childhood on an ice floe, it's also the years of hibernation in Paris and the fall I took while skiing at the Totem into four sets of arms. The wages of my ethnic neurosis are the impact of the *monocoque* and the sheets of steel launched against an unshakable ton of obstacles. From now on I'm exempt from acting coherently and released once and for all from making a success of my life. If I wanted to I could end my days in the muffled torpor of an anhistoric institute, sit indefinitely before ten windows that display unequal portions of a conquered land and await the final judgement when, given the psychiatric evaluation and the extenuating circumstances, surely I'll be acquitted.

And so provided with a legal file and its psychiatric appendix, I can dedicate myself to writing page after page of abolished words laid out in accordance with harmonies that are always pleasant to experience, even though if worse came to worse that could seem like work. But this carefully dosed effort is neither harmful nor contra-indicated, as long as the periods of writing are brief, of course, and followed by periods of rest. Nothing stops the politically depressed from conferring an aesthetic colouring on this verbal secretion; nothing prevents him from transferring to this improvised work the meaning that his own existence lacks, that is absent from his country's future. Yet there's something desperate about this investment of spare funds. It's terrible and I can't hide it from myself any longer: I am desperate. No one had told me that in becoming a patriot I'd be cast into adversity like this or that because I wanted freedom, I'd find myself locked up. How many seconds of dread, how many centuries of impotence must I live before I merit the final embrace of a white sheet? Nothing leads me to believe that a new and wonderful life will replace this one. Condemned to the dark, I hit the walls of a dungeon cell that finally, after thirty-four years of lies, I inhabit fully and in all humiliation. I am a prisoner of my madness, locked up inside my probationary helplessness, crouching over a piece of paper as white as a sheet with which one hangs oneself.

BETWEEN CUBA'S July 26 and the lyric night of August 4, between Place de la Riponne and the pizzeria on Place de l'Hôtel-de-Ville in Lausanne, I met a blonde woman whose majestic stride I recognized at once. The happiness I felt just then echoes in me still as I sit at a table in this pizzeria – meeting-place for the masons of Tessin – and give in to the sadness that's been numbing me progressively ever since I left my hotel, where all I did was spend some unproductive minutes after I'd gone to the Benjamin Constant movie theatre. In this pizzeria I ran aground.

And when the jukebox gave off the first chords of "Desafinado" for the third time, I'd had all the nostalgia I could take. To the rhythm of Afro-Brazilian guitars I got up and paid my bill. And here I am again in that earlier night, constricted once more in the vise of the rue des Escaliers-du-Marché, which I climb as if this slope could offset my inner fall. It's a few steps from Place de la Riponne and it was while I was making my way there that I spotted K's leonine mane. I speeded up and was soon beside her, very close to her face, which was turned away. I was afraid my sudden approach would frighten her and so, acting quickly to avert a misunderstanding, I spoke her name with an inflection I was sure she'd recognize. And it was then that the wonderful event, our

16

reunion, occurred, as the two of us were approaching the grand esplanade of Place de la Riponne. We'd turned left after the dark colonnade of the university and the blinding happiness of our reunion. I don't remember what route we followed next or what dark streets we strolled, K and I, before stopping for a moment on the great bridge just above the Gazette de Lausanne facing the dark mass of the cantonal government building that hid Lac Léman and the spectre of the Alps. Twelve months of separation, of misunderstandings and censorship, were ended magically by this coincidence: a few words relearned, the light touch of our bodies, their new expectations. Twelve months of lost love and lassitude were eradicated by the bliss of this unexpected encounter and our fierce love; we were carried away again towards the upper valley of the Nile, drifting voluptuously between Montreal and Toronto, between Queen Mary Road and the Portuguese-Jewish cemetery, from our lyric rooms at the Polytechnical Institute to our fleeting encounters in Pointe-Claire, some time between a violent July 26 and a funereal August 4, twofold anniversary of a twofold revolution: one that began dangerously and the other, secret, that arose from our kisses and our sacrileges.

Our life could be summed up by some sad and voluptuous oaths exchanged one rainy evening in a car parked near the barracks on Île Sainte-Hélène. Before I met you I was writing an endless poem. Then one day I shuddered, knowing you were naked under your clothes; you talked but I only remember your mouth. You talked as you waited, while I simply waited. We were standing, your hair was tangled with an etching of Venice by Clarence Gagnon. That was how I saw Venice, over your shoulder, drowned in your brown eyes while I held you close. I don't need to go to Venice to know that the city resembles your head thrown back against the living-room wall while I held you. Your languor led me to our forbidden embrace, your great dark eyes to your damp hands that searched for my truth. Who are you if not the ultimate woman who sways to the rhythms of desire and my veiled caresses? The seeds of our revolutionary plans were sown in our apostatized pleasure. And now, on a midsummer night, somewhere between old Lausanne and its medieval port, on the median line that separates two days and two bodies, we rediscover our old reason for living and wishing for death a thousand times rather than face up to the cruel separation whose sudden end flooded us with joy.

We walked till late that night, till the entire Rhône valley was filled with sun, and little by little the old port of Ouchy rang out with the sound of motors and work, and the waiters set out the chairs on the terrace of the Hôtel d'Angleterre where, during a single night in the beautiful summer of 1816, Byron wrote "The Prisoner of Chillon." We had breakfast at a table on the hotel terrace, silent beside the liquid mirror still veiled by a hazy breath. After a twelve-month separation, after twelve times measuring the impossibility of living one more month, after a night spent walking from Place de la Riponne to the ancient lake, at the first hour of dawn we went up to a room in the Hôtel d'Angleterre, perhaps the one where Byron sang of Bonnivard, who had once foundered in a cell in the Château de Chillon. K and I, drenched in the same flood of sorrow, lay down naked between cool sheets, annihilated voluptuously by one another in the timely splendour of our poem and the dawn. Again tonight I'm shattered by our blinding embrace, by the incantatory shock of our two bodies, and now, at the end of this blazing dawn, I'm alone on a blank page where I no longer breathe the warm breath of a fair-haired stranger, where I no longer feel her weight that attracts me according to a Copernican system, where I no longer see her amber skin or her tireless lips or her sylvan eyes, where I don't hear the pure song of her pleasure. Alone now in my paginated bed, I ache as I remember that lost time now regained, spent naked in the secret profusion of the pleasures of the flesh.

The swaying rhythms of "Desafinado," which burst unex-
pectedly from the Multivox, raise me up to the level of the
bitter lake where I rediscovered the dawn of your body in one
overwhelming embrace. They take me to your membranous
shore where it would have been better to die because I'm
dying now. The weather that morning was fine, it marked the
exalted union of two days and our two bodies. Yes, it was
absolute dawn, between a July 26 that evaporated above the
lake and the immanent night of the revolution. The burden
of words inside me doesn't stop the clear stream of time past
from cascading into the lake. Past time now passes again,
even more quickly than it did that morning in our room at
the Hôtel d'Angleterre, with its view of the vanished glacier
of Galenstock which descended one day to the very spot on
the hotel terrace where K and I sat at dawn. Vanished glacier,
vanished love, fleeting interglacial dawn, a kiss that has fled
to the far shore, far from the misty window of my bathy-
scaphe that dives beneath the window where Byron wept in
his stanzas to Bonnivard and I in the golden tresses of the
woman I love.

This evening, if I am adrift in the bed of the great soluble
river, if the Hôtel d'Angleterre is breaking up in the liquid
tomb of my memory, if I've stopped hoping for dawn at the
end of the occlusive night, and if everything is collapsing to
the strains of "Desafinado," all this is because I see at the
bottom of the lake the inevitable truth, a terrifying partner
no longer disconcerted by my flights and my displays. In the
watery depths the unnamed enemy who haunts me finds me
naked and defenceless, just as I was in the embrace that
forever confirmed us, K and me, as the elusive owners of the
Hôtel d'Angleterre, located midway between the Château de
Chillon and the Villa Diodati, between Manfred and the
future liberation of Greece. Let the global enemy come, for
I'm pining away as I wait for him! Let the confrontation come,
and the realization of the truth that is threatening me. Or else

let them set me free, now, with no other form: me, a prisoner with no poet to sing of my exploits. Then I'll drown once again in a warm, unmade bed, in the blazing body of the woman who has sated me with love between the night of a chance meeting and a second night, between the dark bottom of Lac Léman and its helical surface. Superfluous words surge past my window, they darken the perimeter of memory and I capsize as I tell my story. Did the meeting at the Hôtel d'Angleterre take place on June 24 or July 26; and is this faltering mass that blocks my field of vision the Montreal Prison or the Château de Chillon, romantic dungeon where the patriot Bonnivard still awaits the revolutionary war I've incited without poetry? Between this lakeside prison and the Villa Diodati near Geneva, in a divine hotel room at a place where Byron once stayed, I reinvented love. I discovered a sun, eclipsed by twelve months of separation, which rose that morning between our united bodies, warming the supreme centre of our bed and bursting forth, resplendent and unbearable, in the ancient lake that tumbled gloriously from our two bellies. If only the room, the sun, and our love could be returned to me, for here I have nothing and I'm afraid. What is happening inside me that makes the alpine granite tremble? The paper slips away beneath my weight, like a lake fed by a river. Insidiously, my depression demineralizes me. From a sea of ice I become greedy lava, mirror of suicide. Thirty pieces of silver and I'd kill myself! I would even drop the price lower to cut myself with a shard of glass and be done with revolutionary depression! Yes, it would mark the end of the conspirator's shameful disease, of mental fracture, of falls perpetrated in a police cell. The end of plans for attack, perpetually renewed, and the indecent pleasure of walking in the crowd of voters as I grip the cool butt of the automatic weapon I wear like a sling! And I'll fly! Let me walk, unknown and unpunished, through the streets that run from Place de la Riponne and wind their way streaming to the shores of Pully and Ouchy, let me mingle with the great current of history and disappear, anonymous and universal, in the powerful river of the revolution!

All that matters to me is the period of time between the night in the upper part of town and the revolutionary dawn that struck our bodies like lightning in a room where Byron spent a night writing, between Clarens and the Villa Diodati, already en route to a revolutionary war which ended in the final epilepsy of Missolonghi. All that matters to me is this road of light and euphoria. And our embrace at dawn, a closely fought battle, long but so precise, that annihilated us both in the same fainting fit, flooding us with the pure blood of violence!

I don't want to live here any more with both feet on the cursed soil. I don't want to endure our national dungeon as if nothing were amiss. I dream of bringing to a permanent stop my drowning, which already dates back several generations. Deep in my polluted river I still feed on foreign bodies, I swallow indifferently the molecules of our secular depressions, and it disgusts me. From generation to generation I fill myself with antibodies. Faithful to our bitter motto, I get drunk on a nitric beverage, and I'm hooked.

IT WAS NEARLY six o'clock when we left our room in the Hôtel d'Angleterre. The sun, source of our love and our intoxication, was already growing hazy behind the Cornets de Bise, draining the great valley of its significance. But in us the star still blazed with its hypnagogic brilliance. We sauntered to the Quai des Belges, nonchalantly joining workers and lovers. Then we went closer to the lake. Drunk with the intoxication of bygone days, we strolled along the big jetty and the wharf. The steamer *Neuchâtel* was moored there, surrounded by a noisy, cheerful crowd. We sat some distance from the white boat and the crowd on the diminishing line of rocks that emerged from the blue water of Lac Léman. If only this landscape would imprison me again in its beautiful improbability, I could die without bitterness! If only I could stroll hand in hand with K again on the shores of Ouchy, if I could totter along these eroded rocks and sit close beside K, so close that her twilight hair would brush my cheek! Because I could be delirious here, with my back to the terraced city as I faced the torn depths of the great nearby mountains, close to the woman, a free spirit, who walked on the water and whom I love! And what did our happiness consist of as we gazed at its darkened glints in the cypresses that camouflaged the steamer *Neuchâtel* in the serene water of the lake and on the great Alps

22

whose dazzling flanks loomed up before us? What had filled this time except perhaps the long and ardent journey that had gone before and the recent explosion of our pleasure: twelve months and one night of falling between Place de la Riponne and the revolutionary dawn that overwhelmed the sky, the whole chain of the Alps, visible and invisible, and our bodies reunited in 1816. While we were becoming the epicentre of a grandiose universe, a consummate serenity followed the laceration of pleasure. At this moment, on these rocks spared by erosion and in the midst of our dizziness, there were no obstacles to my euphoria: I was adrift in plenitude, invested with love and the dawn. Something glorious was at work in me, while the exhausted sun was descending with the waters of the Rhône and K, chilly or perhaps melancholy, moved tenderly close to me.

Then we went back to the darkened city. We took a few steps towards the Hôtel d'Angleterre, stopping before we reached its crowded terrace. We took a table on the terrace of the Château d'Ouchy, turning our backs on the fading sun, looking out on our left at the coastline with its grand hotels and on our right at the gloomy Alps adrift on the lake. It was at that same table, over a gin and tonic and with the grand perspective of the Lepontine Alps sweeping to infinity, that K told me about the Mercedes 300SL with Zurich plates. Lost in K's black eyes, I had trouble following her complicated revelations, especially because I was gazing, thrilled, at her full lips and delighting in her long sentences that were often enigmatic, though they were familiar to me.

"He's a banker," she said to me.

"What's his name again?"

"Carl von Ryndt. But of course you can't trust it. He's a banker like thousands of other Swiss. In Basel a few months ago he was calling himself de Heute or de Heutz. He claimed to be Belgian (he even affected the accent) and that he was writing a thesis on Scipio Africanus . . ."

"Mystifying!"

"But listen to this! Pierre – the boss, that is – had him followed, which wasn't easy with a bird like him. I'll spare you the historical theories he was basing his thesis on. There's something frightening, believe me, about giving yourself a cover like that: it's nearly as complicated as trying to pass as an apostolic nuncio and actually saying a pontifical mass complete with deacons and the rest . . . In any event, von Ryndt couldn't surprise me any more. In Basel he was so successful at passing himself off as a historian of the Roman wars that he actually gave scholarly lectures on Scipio Africanus. We know now that von Ryndt is supposedly writing a thesis that was actually written a hundred years ago by some famous man nobody's ever heard of! He spends less time in the university library than in the annex of the Federal Palace in Berne, claiming he's doing research in the federal capital: for a long time von Ryndt played a Belgian historian, very studious and specializing in a generally unknown period of Roman history. By the end of our investigation, de Heute or de Heutz – von Ryndt's double, that is – proved to be incredibly shrewd and downright dangerous for us . . . You know, since my separation I've looked at things more coldly than I used to. To tell the truth, I changed my philosophy of life by making a mess of my own . . . What are you thinking about? You look so sad suddenly . . . Disaster doesn't frighten me any more. I don't think I'll ever live through another period as bleak as the past twelve months, which I spent in hotel rooms in Manchester, London, Brussels, Berne, or Geneva, in transit in all those cities and obliged to keep up a bold front. I think I went through a severe depression: I was on medication for a while, but I've never gone for treatment. Now it's over. How do I seem to you? Look how wonderful it is on the lake just now. If I were a millionaire, I'd buy a villa here on the shore of the lake. And when I was depressed, I wouldn't budge from my villa. I'd just stay there and look at the mountains, the way we're doing right now . . ."

"It's wonderful around Vevey. Do you know Clarens? No . . . Or maybe on the shore between St-Prex and Allaman – but I'm dreaming too. We'll never be millionaires unless we make off with the funds of the organization and pull some successful holdups . . . But if I ever made a million, I wouldn't sink my capital into a Swiss chalet. I'd rather open an account at the Fabrique Nationale or Solingen . . ."

"You're right. There's no golden retirement for us, not even a peaceful life as long as we can't live normally in our country. Tonight, I'm in Lausanne. In a few days the organization will send me somewhere else . . ."

I was lost in her gaze, a black lake where just that morning I had seen the sun emerge, bare and flamboyant. I was sad with K's sadness, happy when she seemed happy, and I became a revolutionary again when she alluded to the revolution that had brought us together and that still obsesses me, unfinished . . .

"Over the past six months, he's been seen in Montreal three times as far as we know. We have proof that he's in contact with Gaudy and that this von Ryndt (or the Belgian) is Gaudy's emissary in Europe. Now do you understand?"

"I understand . . . and at this point I wouldn't wait one second more to accept the obvious, I'd swing into action. It's just that while we're talking about von Ryndt, he may have changed his name yet again . . ."

K gave me a long look that was both defiant and loving. We understood one another, and she went on quite simply:

"We have to settle this problem in the next twenty-four hours . . . Don't you agree? But let me tell you a little more about him. Von Ryndt is president of the Banque Commerciale Saharienne at 13 or 14 rue Bonnivard in Geneva. He's also on the board of the Union des Banques Suisses. I'll pass over the relationship between the UBS and the Berne Secret Service. But you know that the UBS is a powerful federal lobby, and you also know that article 47b of the federal constitution, which guarantees anonymity to anyone using Switzerland as a safety deposit box, may, at a certain level and very discreetly, break the rules. When you get right down to it, von Ryndt is a visionary who knows about certain secret funds, the organization's for instance, and who can therefore freeze them simply by eliminating the few patriots with legal access to them. It's even possible that whenever a deposit is made into a Swiss bank account, there's a duplicate that through von Ryndt is deposited in RCMP files in Ottawa, in Montreal, and maybe even with our 'friends' the CIA. And as every foreigner's stay on Swiss soil is recorded in meticulous detail, by working methodically von Ryndt and his colleagues can know which of us is making the transfers and so forth . . ."

"Carl von Ryndt, Banque Commerciale Saharienne, 13 rue Bonnivard, Mercedes 300SL with Zurich plates. I'll remember that. But does this Banque Commerciale Saharienne really exist, or is it like our Laboratoire de Recherches Pharmacologiques SA?"

K gave me all the co-ordinates of the man with the powerful car that would soon be of no use to him. Then around six-thirty p.m. we separated, after arranging to meet twenty-four hours later on the terrace of the Hôtel d'Angleterre under the window of the room we'd just left, drunk on each other, in love.

NOW THAT IT'S well past my deadline, I'm trying to recall, in order, the minutes between the time when I left K at the Château d'Ouchy and the next day when I went back to the terrace of the Hôtel d'Angleterre, but I keep getting lost in this official report. I skid on the hairpin turns of memory just as my Volvo continued to skid on the Col des Mosses between Aigle and Etibaz before I came back to Château d'Oex. My first information about von Ryndt took me to the Hôtel des Trois Rois in Vevey, and from there I went to the Rochers de Naye at Montreux, still looking for the banker with the 300SL. According to the bellhop I smoothed over with Swiss francs, von Ryndt was going to meet a notary called Rubattel in Château d'Oex, on the Chemin du Temple near Schwub's pharmacy. I figured it would take me an hour to drive from the heart of Montreux to Château d'Oex if I pushed it. But I stepped on my Volvo's gas pedal hard enough to warp the sheet of steel under my feet. Traffic between Montreux and Yvorne was heavy and it was unbelievably hard to stay on schedule. In my Volvo, stuck in the demoralizing stream of cars, I felt as if time were working against me, and I was certain that von Ryndt was living out his final hours in the offices of the Union Fribourgeoise de Crédit. I tried hard to pass the fools ahead of me who were doing sixty kilometres an hour. I was struggling at the wheel, sweating so much that my shirt was soaked under my left armpit, where I could feel the weight of my Colt 38 automatic, firmly sheathed in its holster. Before I drove into Aigle, I literally leapt onto the bypass road on the way to Sepey and Saanen. As soon as I'd left the Pont de la Grande Eau, I switched on my high-beams and drove at breakneck speed along the steep wall of the mountain. At the first hairpin turn I realized that the car was straining on its axle. But as I climbed towards the Diablerets, I continued to take each curve at maximum speed, reducing my ties to the ground to a plaintive squeal. At every turn I reduced the slim margin separating me from a swerve – a bold procedure that gained me a few seconds.

Time passes and I take forever to cross the Col des Mosses. Each turn surprises me in third gear when I should have already started to gear down; each sentence disconcerts me. I burn words, stages, memories, and I keep freeing myself from the tracery of this interpolated night. The event that's already too far ahead of me will unfold shortly, in a few minutes, when I arrive at the trough of the valley and the essential level of my double life. This winding road that flies past in my high-beams suddenly slows down before I get to Château d'Oex. The asphalt ribbon that weaves between Les Mosses and Le Tornettaz brings me here, close to the Cartierville bridge and the Montreal Prison, less than a fifteen-minute drive from my legal domicile and my private life. All the curves I passionately embrace and the valleys I escort bring me inevitably into this stifling pen populated by ghosts. I want out of here. I'm afraid of getting used to this shrunken space; I'm afraid that greedily drinking in the impossible will change me, and that when I'm set free I won't be able to walk on my own two feet. I'm afraid of waking up degenerated, stripped of identity, annihilated. Someone who isn't me, with eyes wild and brain purged of any antecedent, will walk through the gate on the day of my liberation. My pain is too exhausting to let me experience, to try to designate the slightest relief. That, no doubt, is why, whenever I gather momentum in this choppy narrative, I immediately forget why I've been pursuing it. I can't help thinking that my written race in the shadow of Les Mosses and Le Tornettaz is a futile one, when I remind myself that I'm a prisoner here in an unassailable cage. I spend my time encoding passwords, as if I were eventually going to escape! I streamline my sentences so they'll take flight sooner! I send my proxy by Volvo into the Col des Mosses, help him reach the upper level of the pass without a hitch, and send him racing down the other side of the mountain at hair-raising velocity, thinking that the higher speed will have an effect on me and let me avoid a spiral fall into an unmoving ditch. Everything breaks free here except me. Words slip by, and time, the Alpine landscape, and the Vaudois villages, while I, I shudder in my immanence and perform a dance of possession inside a prescribed circle.

At Château d'Oex, the clock in the steeple shows half-past eight when, after an hour of investigation between the offices of the Union Fribourgeoise de Crédit and the villa of the Pastors of the National Church, I set off again along the same road but in the opposite direction, looking not for the president of the Banque Commerciale Saharienne but for a Belgian citizen fascinated by Roman history and with a mandate to make trouble for us. The 300SL had vanished somewhere between Montreux and the Pastors of the National Church. According to official sources, Scipio Africanus was travelling in a blue Opel – more appropriate for a university professor. My information came from Pastor Nussbaumer, himself a specialist in the historiography of the Sonderbund. After identifying myself as a specialist in the Punic wars, I questioned him subtly. As God is my witness, I was quite surprised to learn through this subterfuge about the presence in Switzerland of a colleague who knew Scipio Africanus like the back of his hand. My conversation with Pastor Nussbaumer boosted my morale and put me in great shape for climbing the darkened wall of the Mosses in one go, which I did with a briskness and precision that could have qualified me for the Rallye des Alpes. Once I'd reached the highest point of the pass, I didn't give myself a moment's respite: I floored the gas pedal along the only straight part of the road and, at the end, stepped on the brake before gearing down to take on the first of a long series of turns. From parabola through ellipse and double S-curve, I get to the Sepey and then all the way to the Rhône in the vicinity of Aigle. In nineteen minutes and twelve seconds – timing unofficial but accurate – I travelled the distance between Les Charmilles, where I'd seen the Reverend Nussbaumer, and the cog-railway station just outside Aigle. I was proud, and rightly so, of my schuss performance and of the way my Volvo hugged the road.

Enthusiastically and with sensational style, I travelled the last leg between me and the famous Professor H. de Heutz. From Aigle to the Château de Chillon I drove like a maniac and then, after a bottleneck outside Montreux-Vevey, I set off again for the gates of the beloved city of Lausanne, driving through it blindly. Around ten o'clock I slowed down: I was finally in Geneva. Taking the road to Lausanne had brought me to the Quai des Bergues and I drove along it, breaking every one of this Calvinist country's traffic laws. Then, after crossing the Rhône at the very spot where the Helvetians would have crossed if they hadn't been wiped out by Caesar, I went down several streets and arrived, fresh as a daisy, at the door of the Société d'Histoire de la Suisse Romande. My Swiss-made watch showed twelve minutes past ten.

"Excuse me, Madame, is this where Professor de Heutz is lecturing . . . ?"

"You're too late, Monsieur. Surely you don't think at this hour of the night . . ."

"Do you know where he might be, by any chance? I'm a colleague . . ."

"Geneva's a big city. You can always try, but where? I suggest you get in touch with Monsieur Bullinger, our president. He often drops by the Café du Globe after our lectures . . ."

A few minutes later I was parked diagonally on the Quai du Général-Guisan near the Globe. I was amazed to realize that the lecture on "Caesar and the Helvetians," which I'd promised myself to attend when I was drinking a beer in Vevey, had been given in my absence by the man I'd been pursuing from one canton to the next.

The Globe terrace was still all lit up and crowded. Inside, I could make out the silhouettes of other customers and waiters. Before going into action, I pretended for a while that I was just hanging around and looked in jewellers' windows till I spotted a blue Opel parked across from the café. From a seat on the terrace, I could keep an eye on the car; then, after its owner had gone inside, I'd still have time to get to my Volvo, parked a little further away, and chase the Opel. Once I was sitting over a Feldschlossen with a thick head of foam, I reviewed the situation. Pastor Nussbaumer knew that I wanted to meet H. de Heutz, as did the receptionist at the Société d'Histoire de la Suisse Romande: both had every reason to believe that I was also a colleague and friend of H. de Heutz. (In case I made a mess of things, my Volvo would head for Italy and I'd go back to playing a Canadian Press correspondent in Switzerland, domiciled at 18 boulevard James-Fazy, Geneva.) Furthermore, the Belgian historian has nothing to do with the banker Carl von Ryndt, whose disappearance would surely be of no concern to Pastor Nussbaumer or to the honourable members of the Société d'Histoire de la Suisse Romande or even to the waiter who'd brought me my beer. Of course the bellhop at the Rochers de Naye in Montreux knew that a man corresponding vaguely to my anthropometric record was looking for a man named von Ryndt and was getting ready to travel from Montreux to Château d'Oex to meet him. But that bellhop, who was as discreet as a banker, would only be able to assert that I hadn't found my man at Château d'Oex because, in any event, I'd stopped looking for von Ryndt at Château d'Oex and had begun, after metamorphosing into a Romanist, to look for one H. de Heutz, acknowledged expert on Scipio Africanus and Caesar's wars. On the terrace of the Café du Globe, three customers were airing their scholarly opinions about Balzac in pure native Genevan accents.

"You know Simenon's theory? Fascinating, absolutely fascinating. He maintains that Balzac may have been impotent ..."

"But that theory has two flaws, dear friend: first, it's completely unverifiable; and second, it's inconsistent with the facts. Remember Balzac's affair with Madame Hanska ... That happened right here in Geneva – and not on paper! Their subsequent correspondence contains precise references to their amorous meetings in Geneva ..."

"But that's just it, it was his use of verbal extravaganzas to describe simple meetings that Simenon thought were fishy. Once a man has possessed a woman, he no longer needs to write to her in the persuasive mode. One persuades the woman first ..."

"Unless a man has left a woman with child, there's always room to suspect impotence. It's a terrible nuisance ..."

"I also find it hard to believe that Geneva was harmful to Balzac and that it was in our city that he experienced such a humiliation. It's nothing to be proud of. As well as the fact that this unfortunate rumour would be bad for tourism ..."

There was a burst of laughter at the other table while I rested from my mad race by gazing at the inert space of the lake, waiting to kill the time of a man of whom all I knew was his ability to change identities. What wonderful moments I spent on that terrace, waiting for one of my numerous neighbours to get up and go to the blue Opel parked along the Quai du Général-Guisan. Geneva struck me as the pleasantest spot in the world for a terrorist to wait for the man he's going to kill. Antechamber of revolution and anarchy, the ancient city constricted by the Rhône enchanted me because of its sweetness, its nocturnal calm, and its lights reflected in the lake. I felt great, even wonderful. My thoughts were flying off in every direction.

I could see Balzac sitting where I was seated as he dreamed up the *Story of the Thirteen*, ecstatically imagining an elusive and pure Ferragus, conferring on the fictitious *übermensch* the powers that, according to my nameless neighbours, had been cruelly lacking in the novelist himself. The triumphal potency of Ferragus avenged his own shameful debacle, and the virile action that lit up those blazing pages stood in for acts that had not taken place in a melancholy bed in the Hôtel d'Arc or somewhere else. Ferragus haunted me that evening in this city that had treated the novelist badly; Balzac's fictitious and enigmatic avenger slowly entered me, inhabiting me as a secret society might infiltrate a corrupt city, transforming it into a citadel. The shadow of the great Ferragus shielded me, his blood injected an inflammable substance into my veins: I too was ready to avenge Balzac no matter what by draping myself in his character's black cape.

I was ready to strike, impatient even, when I saw two silhouettes cross the street and go up to the blue Opel parked across from the lake. In the time it took me to drop a few Swiss francs on the table, H. de Heutz had opened the Opel's door. I was at the wheel of my Volvo and I'd started it when H. de Heutz's car began to move rather slowly along the Quai du Général-Guisan. Despite the distance I kept between the Opel and me, I saw that there was a woman with him. The road H. de Heutz took was fairly complicated, travelling along nearly deserted streets that posed problems of discretion for me; finally he parked on Place Simon-Goulart, which fortunately I was familiar with, so I was able to park unnoticed. From a distance I saw him get out of the car with the woman; they started slowly along the sidewalk, arm in arm, heading for the Quai des Bergues. I followed them, careful not to attract their attention. In any case, my dear expert on Scipio Africanus wasn't behaving like a hunted man. I was unsure what to make of the woman whose arm he was holding, nor did I know how to put her inside the parentheses of zero hour. I was still thinking about it when events compelled me to linger unwisely over the movements of the clocks displayed in every shop window. Then, at the corner of rue du Mont-Blanc, the woman disappeared as if by magic, making me realize that her departure was even more puzzling than her cumbersome presence; H. de Heutz continued strolling, his pace more agile now. In fact, he was going much too quickly for me. I found it hard to follow him without adopting his hurried rhythm and thus attracting attention.

I'd have been better off staying in the Volvo and tailing him in peace. Too late now to retrace my steps. There was something unrealistic, insane about this nighttime stroll. H. de Heutz and I were proceeding towards the Carouge neighbourhood, once a refuge for Russian revolutionaries, almost at a run. H. de Heutz was leading me despite myself into the river of the great revolution. And while I was dreaming of the famous exiles who had roamed the narrow, desperate streets of Carouge long before us, just when I least expected it, I took a blow on my back and another, harder one on my neck. A crack developed in the Geneva night, and I felt I was being manipulated by a great many skilful hands.

THE ROOM I was in was magnificent: three big French windows opened onto a charming garden, and at the very end of the landscape, a shimmering surface that made me think I was still in Switzerland, in a salon, what's more – and what a salon! I was fascinated by the large armoire with its marquetry angel figures, wood on wood. Perfectly stunning. Mechanically, I asked:

"Where am I?"

"At the chateau."

"Which chateau?"

"The chateau of Versailles, idiot."

"Ah . . ."

Little by little I was emerging from a comatose sleep and at the same time becoming aware of a throbbing pain in the back of my neck, which immediately drove away the amnesia from which I'd been suffering. I realized that the night was over. Twenty-four hours had elapsed since dawn in the Hôtel d'Angleterre. I was lost, truly lost and – this I realized when I made an automatic move – unarmed.

"So your mind is working again?"

The man stood facing me with his back to the light so that I couldn't make out his face. But I realized that he knew what he was talking about and that if I wanted to have a useful exchange with him, I'd better get my wits back as quickly as possible.

"I'd like a glass of water . . ."

"Here there is nothing to drink but champagne . . . So we're playing spy, are we? Wandering around at night with a gun, pursuing honest taxpaying citizens who have all their papers in order? What a disgrace for Switzerland."

"I think there's been a misunderstanding."

"If that's so, you'd better start explaining . . ."

I had to be quick and confident or I'd never be able to pull myself out of this faux pas. I needed to think up a quick retort, and since I no longer had a weapon to draw, I'd have to empty my dialectical magazine on this stranger who was standing between me and the daylight. Alas, the seconds of silence that were mounting up restored neither my reflexes nor my presence of mind. My speech was still slurred and I couldn't even reason clearly in the hope of resuming control of the situation. Right now I can't even whisper to my double the formulaic remarks that would get him out of this jam. The other man's para-helical silhouette is blocking me; outrageously, he fills the entire landscape where I dream confusedly of running along streams to the enchanting lake. I'm paralyzed by something that resembles a thrombosis; and I can't take myself out of the national catatonia that has me frozen here on a Louis xv armchair – or maybe it's Regency – before a placid stranger who doesn't even know what I'm doing in his life, whereas I, who know all too well, have to silence him and above all, yes, above all, and as soon as possible, come up with another explanation, improvise on the spot a scenario that will get me out of this place . . .

"I want to see your superior," I tell him.

"It's un-Christian to disturb someone this early in the morning . . ."

"I don't care, I have to see him. I'm on an official mission and I have to know whom I'm dealing with before I disclose my identity. I'm serious: be quick, it's very important . . . for you. In fact . . . I have a feeling that we're in the same line of business and, besides, that we work for the same interests . . ."

There were many drawbacks to making the first move, especially because I didn't know yet if my adversary had a clear picture of why I'd shadowed him the night before. I had to proceed cautiously and dissemble with style or I was liable to be taken unawares. The memory of the ruined evening that saw my elaborate race from the Château d'Ouchy to the Hôtel des Rochers de Naye in Montreux, then my round trip across the Col des Mosses to Château d'Oex with a stop in Geneva where I practised my running, was bitterly humiliating. While drawing on all the resources of my pride as I tried to look intelligent, I was still obsessed by my failure. The worst humiliation was still to come because, in a few hours, if I should be set free, I'd have to show K how ineffectual I'd been, give her a detailed account: my automobile exploit, my euphoria on the terrace of the Café du Globe, and my final rout. All things considered, I was disqualified by H. de Heutz, and if I'm now steering clear of a detailed review of my mission, it's so I won't twist the knife in the wound.

My armed guard was standing motionless between the windows while I, rotting with shame and impatience, stood against the light from the vast, extra-luminous landscape that spread out beyond the chateau. How to adopt a haughty attitude when all you want to do is cry and use the telephone, as if that were something to do in such a situation? Anyway, I didn't have K's number, and the only way we'd agreed to get in touch was to meet on the terrace of the Hôtel d'Angleterre late that afternoon. In the meantime, in return for such a display of imagination and boldness I had only one thing to do: leave the leaden chateau where an unknown man, H. de Heutz no doubt, was letting the butt of his 45 protrude from his jacket and, not without elegance, questioning me and forcing me to answer before I'd got my wits back. He interrogated me, and there was no question of not answering: it would have been impolite and awkward and it would have prolonged an incarceration that as far as my honour was concerned had already lasted too long. So I reply after a fashion. I speak, but what do I actually say? I don't make any sense. My improvised remarks veer into insinuations. Why in hell should I recount this tangled tale about my office in Geneva and tell him that a phone call would set matters straight and bring this ridiculous misunderstanding to an end? I'm talking nonsense.

It's painful, this conversation with me at the centre. I keep it from flagging, I say whatever comes into my head, I unwind the bobbin, I make connections, I cause no end of trouble. Then I really go overboard, tell him I'm having a nervous breakdown, try to look as if I'm high on drugs. And all this business about financial problems, the tall tale about my two children and my wife whom I've abandoned: a pack of lies . . . He still hasn't moved. If he hasn't slapped me, it may be because he's taken the bait. Maybe I've even given him a good show. I make a last-ditch effort and go on telling my implausible story . . .

"I've been showing off for a while now; I'm trying to stand up and play the game. This business about an armed chase and espionage is a gruesome joke. The truth is simpler: two weeks ago I abandoned my wife and my two children . . . I don't have the strength to go on living: I've lost my mind . . . In fact, I was heading for disaster, awash in debts, and I couldn't do a thing, couldn't even go home. I panicked: I took off, ran away like a coward . . . I'd intended to use the pistol in a holdup, make off with several thousand Swiss francs. I went into many banks, gripping the weapon, but I could never use it. I was afraid. Last night I walked all over Geneva – I don't even remember where; I was looking for a deserted spot . . . to commit suicide! [All is well: H. de Heutz hasn't moved a muscle yet.] I want to end it. I don't want to live any longer . . ."

"Sure. That's pretty hard to swallow . . ."

"You don't have to believe me. At this point I couldn't care less."

"If you insist on killing yourself, it's your business . . . But I'm not explaining myself very well: if you had the urge to do that in the middle of the night, why start tailing a man and not let him out of your sight?"

"But I wasn't following you; I don't even know you . . . Aha, so that's why I'm here! Now I understand . . . My life is over in any case, so do what you want. You thought I was a spy: do what you have to do in such a case. Kill me. I'm asking you to . . ."

I was somewhat surprised to see that H. de Heutz almost believed my psychiatric rendition. One thing is certain though, he hesitated. Meanwhile, I was putting on the mask of a severely depressed man. I was thinking about the two young children waiting for me somewhere and about their mother who couldn't tell them why Papa doesn't sleep at home any more. Poor kids, they won't even know that their father wanted to kill himself because he lacked the strength to remake his life or to rob banks. They don't know that their father is disreputable, a degenerate. While I think about these expectant children, something unpleasant is going on inside me. Wanting to be taken for someone else has made me into that other person; suddenly the two children he abandoned are mine, and I'm ashamed. H. de Heutz is still looking at me. I slump down before him. I've swallowed whatever dignity I have. I no longer have even the old pride that used to let me eject myself from a flaming vehicle. I'm prisoner in a chateau that faces the blazing lake whose glimmers I can distinguish at the back of the landscape. Through the big windows light floods in and fills the opulent salon where I'm dying of lethargy and helplessness, ensconced in my invented depression. I no longer know what's going to happen and I don't even feel like maintaining the initiative to keep H. de Heutz from outdistancing me.

"And what's this, a love letter?"

He unfolds a sheet of blue paper, the same one I found in my mail at the Hôtel de la Paix the other evening. He holds out the paper without moving the barrel of his gun away from my face. At once, I recognize the shape of that damned poem. I scan it again, not trying to decipher it but thinking it was a piece of evidence: CINBEUPERFLEUDIARUNCOBES-CUBEREBESCUAZURANOCTIVAGUS. While I murmured each syllable of this cryptogram, I told myself that I was finished because of this abstract message that may actually have been nothing but a huge joke on the part of Hamidou, dear man, a transcription into Latin characters of some vernacular dirty joke. Good old Hamidou had got me in a fine fix with his secret message: my time is definitely up, my goose is cooked, I'm kaput, versich! Nevertheless, to me the stream of syllables in that hypercoded message meant that I had better things to do than try to gain some time when time itself was working against me. The seconds were breaking into a thousand divergent hunches that wouldn't lead to any precise action. I'd have to put an end to this rush of pointless hunches soon, and do something besides gawk at H. de Heutz and at the horrible Senegalese stomach rumble which I was trying to read between the lines, as if a signal might come to me from this sticky pile of consonants and vowels that was nothing but a brilliant example of black humour.

Far below in the valley the glacial lake was glinting and the morning sun was starting its fiery course around the Aiguille du Géant when suddenly, with a slowness that reassured me about the acuity of my reflexes, I held out the sheet of paper to H. de Heutz, who made a move with his left arm to take it back. It would have been too easy, therefore awkward, to attack him just then when all his muscles were tensed to fend off a surprise. I gave him time to fold up Hamidou's message and get far enough ahead of me to feel secure. Which he did, sure that if I'd had to attack I'd have done so when the distance between us was minimal and our hands were nearly touching. Now that he'd moved away from me, H. de Heutz relaxed and visibly loosened up his defence system. I slowly shifted my feet into the starting position; then, inside the infinitesimal crack of hesitation, I leaped to his right and hit his temple as hard as I could, hard enough to throw him off balance and interrupt the move he'd begun to make, to draw his weapon, which he'd carelessly put back in the holster after regaining possession of the blue paper. My right arm made the move that his was supposed to make, and I grabbed the butt of his revolver. Then I moved as if to ward him off, which put a screen of distance between us and allowed me to fire.

"One word and I shoot. Go out ahead of me. Take me to the car . . ."

I followed close behind him, concentrating on his movements so that all I saw of the sumptuous chateau were some fragmented images that my own movements distorted: gilded mouldings, the outline of a buffet, a leather-bound book . . . The chateau remained deep in silence: for my safety, nothing else mattered. On the left, in a vestibule next to the salon, was the exit. We went out quickly to the garden. I let my host get several steps ahead of me to be sure that he was in my sights and to forestall any surprise. I spotted the blue Opel right away: I made him give me the keys and took several steps around the car. Without haste I opened the trunk and gestured to H. de Heutz to get inside; fortunately there was room. He hesitated, surprised and suspicious too, most likely. But since I emphasized my point with a simple movement of the hand holding the gun, he stepped over the rear bumper and curled up inside as best he could just before I brought the lid down. A few seconds later I was at the wheel. I had no trouble starting the Opel's engine and making the little sedan move along the gravel. There was no fence at the exit to the grounds; I turned right instinctively, just in case. The chateau was close to a village that gradually came into sight in my rear-view mirror as I drove away. I spotted a sign on the other side of the little road and slowed down to read the name of the village: Echandens. This name meant nothing to me, but from the configuration of the landscape I guessed I was somewhere between Geneva and Lausanne, closer to Lausanne actually, because of my position relative to the constellation of glaciers that were lit obliquely by the sun. There was just one thing for me to do: drive towards the great depression where, far below, I saw the luminous face of Lac Léman.

TONIGHT, AS I drive between Echandens and the bottom of a valley in the car belonging to a man who's no longer bothering me, I feel discouraged. I have not yet killed this man, H. de Heutz or von Ryndt, and that's depressing. I'm very weary: a vague yearning for suicide has come back to me. I'm tired finally. And my problem strangely resembles that of the unknown man curled up in the trunk of a blue Opel that I drove at a good clip from Echandens to Morges down unfamiliar secondary roads. Now I had just one concern: what method should I use for killing H. de Heutz? As I made my way through this peaceful countryside, I could make out more clearly the cirque of mountains surrounding the lake and recognize the dramatic configuration of this landscape that had enchanted K and me. Emerging onto the heights of Morges, I drove onto the long ribbon of the expressway to Geneva. The dashboard clock read half-past nine; my watch, which was more precise, showed nine-thirty-two. All was well. The package in my trunk didn't reduce my cruising speed. I was genuinely happy, nearly ecstatic as I drove along. My imagination and my superiority had pulled me out of an awkward situation. My honour was safe. At half-past six I would meet K on the terrace of the Hôtel d'Angleterre, which gave me plenty of time to send a few bullets into my passenger's temple. In fact I had too much time: I had practically nothing to do before our meeting and I was already burning with impatience. Overwhelmed as I was, I also felt extravagantly free, inordinately powerful – invincible! Driving into Geneva, I went automatically to Place Simon-Goulart. At once I spotted the egg-like shape of my Volvo. I found a place to park the Opel near the Banque Arabe. In the euphoria of my escape I'd forgotten to think, but now I was suddenly aware of danger. No sooner had I parked than I decided to clear out. First of all, Place Simon-Goulart is not a place where you can easily kill a man in the trunk of a car without rousing suspicion. And some of H. de Heutz's friends might drop by, wait for me to pick up my Volvo, and nab me. I'd been careless.

For some time now I've been awash in melancholy. Fleeting images are all around me, flying in my mental jungle like anopheles. I'm in pain. Hours and hours have been added to the time when I'll kill H. de Heutz. And a cloistered life marks with despair the words imprinted on my broken memory. This republican ennui is cruelly draining me of my revolutionary zeal. Though I don't want to glorify the happiness I've lost, I secretly praise it and confer plenipotentiary attributes on what is not happening to me. I see myself again sitting on the gallery of our rented villa. We were drinking a wine from Johannesburg at the high altitude, facing the Chamossaire; across the valley the great Alps stretched out towards the south. What terrifies me is that I'm no longer suspended in the majestic void; I am here, slipping into the variable densities of my defeat. The passing hours are burying me in despair. I feel so far removed from my former life and from those mornings in Leysin when I would walk in the pure air 1,800 metres above sorrow and failure, well beyond the surface of Lac Léman where, for days now, I've been descending, asphyxiated, into an imaginary current that runs past the terrace of the Hôtel d'Angleterre where I am dying of love. Sensitive only to the movement of the water that pushes me along dazzling shores and makes me glide beneath the base of the Alps, I let it carry me. My past is disembowelled by the hypocritical pressure of the verb. I am dying, drugged, in a false-bottomed lake while I spy through translucent portholes a gelatinous and protozoan mass that exhausts me and resembles me.

In a few days of summer, during that interval between two dwindling shores and two days of revolution, between the flaming island and the frenzied night of August 4, after two centuries of melancholy and thirty-four years of helplessness I am becoming depersonalized. Time is fleeting as I write, everything is becoming a little more rooted, and here I am, dear love, reduced to my final dust. Total mineralization. Motionless, I attain a volcanic stasis. With this historic dust I surround my eyes and eyebrows; I make myself a mask. I write to you.

Writing is a great expression of love. Writing used to mean writing to you; but now that I've lost you I still mass words together, mechanically, because in my heart of hearts I hope that my intellectual wanderings, which I reserve for born debaters, will make their way to you. Then my book of ideas will be simply the cryptic continuation of a night of love with you, my absolute partner to whom I can write in secret by addressing myself to a readership that will never be anything more than the multiplication of your eyes. Writing to you, I address the world. Love is the cycle of the word. I write to you infinitely, endlessly inventing the canticle I read in your eyes; through my words I place my lips on the blazing flesh of my country and I love you, desperately, as on the day of our first communion.

NEXT DAY. Sadness strikes me, as violent and sudden as a lone wave breaking, crashing down on me like a tsunami. Just moments before the commotion I was taking a pleasant trip through my memory, recalling the villages we'd driven through in the Eastern Townships between Acton Vale and Tingwick, which is now called Chénier. Suddenly I'd been struck down, carried away with the trees and my memories at the speed of that cruel wave, swept along in the decanted vomit of our national history, devastated by gloom. The fragile edifice I'd patiently erected to help me face up to hours of seclusion has developed cracks in all its girders, twisting and engulfing me as it is crushed. The only thing that's left for me in this world is to notate my elementary fall. Sorrow sullies me: I pump it in, I swallow it through all my pores, I'm filled with it like a drowned man. Is it obvious that I am aging by myself, that neither the sun nor the pleasures of the flesh now gild my skin? No amorous expectation fills my body; I have no obsessions. I take a few steps down the corridor of my closed submersible; I look through the periscope. I no longer see Cuba's profile foundering above me, or the proud jagged summit of the Grand Combin, or the dreamy silhouette of Byron, or that of my love who waits for me tonight at half-past six on the terrace of the Hôtel d'Angleterre.

Though I draw the tangled thread of my lifeline on this paper, it does not bring back the bed strewn with coloured cushions where we loved each other one June 24, while somewhere beneath our tumult an entire people, gathered together, seemed to be celebrating the irresistible descent of the blood in our veins. You were beautiful, my love. How proud I am of your beauty! How it rewards me! What triumph there was in us that night! What violent and sweet foretaste of the national revolution was unfolding on that narrow bed awash in colours and our two bodies naked, blazing, united in their rhythmic madness. Again tonight my lips hold the damp taste of your boundless kisses. On your bed of chalky sand and on your slippery Alps I descend posthaste, I spread like ground water, I seep in everywhere; an absolute terrorist, I enter all the pores of your spoken lake: I burst, spilling over above the line of your lips, and I flee, oh how I flee, as rapidly as lightning at sea, I flee at the speed of the breaking waves! I topple you, my love, onto this bed suspended above a *fête nationale* ... To think that at this moment I am writing out the minutes of the time we spent outside that insurrectional bed, away from our overwhelming spasm and the dazzling explosion of our desire! I write to fill the time I'm wasting here, that's ruining me, leaving on my face the furrowed traces of its endless alluvium and the indelible proof that I've been eradicated. I write to stave off sorrow and to feel it. Hopelessly I write a long love letter — but when will you read it and when will we be together again and then again? What are you doing at this moment, my love? Where are you travelling outside the walls? Are you moving away from your house, from our memories? Do you sometimes enter the erogenous zone of our *fête nationale*? Do you sometimes kiss me in that stirring chamber crowded with a million disarmed brothers? Do you rediscover the taste of my mouth in the same way that I return obsessively to our kiss and the very fracas of our embrace? Do you think about me? Do you still know my name? Do you hear me deep inside you when your dreaming evocation of our caresses brings a shudder to your sleeping body? Do you look for me in your bed, along your gleaming thighs? Look, I lie full length on you, like the mighty river I flow into your great valley. Endlessly, I draw nearer to you . . .

Words learned, words silenced, our bodies naked at the national solstice, our bodies struck down as they emerged from a caress and the last snow of winter slowed our fall, everything around me is shaken in a crisis of depreciation, as though we were approaching a global conflict. The storm that rages in the financial section strikes my very heart: morbid inflation makes me swell, overflow. I'm afraid, terribly afraid. What will happen to me? I've felt helpless ever since Bakunin's death in a common prison in Berne, awash in debt and forgotten. Revolution, where are you? Are you sinking in flames in the middle of Lac Léman, absurd sun that sheds no light on the depths where I'm making my way, incognito? . . . Between July 26 and my inflationary night, I keep inventing the arms of the woman I love and celebrating through the weary repetition of my prose the prophetic anniversary of our revolution. I keep coming back to this torrid room. Beneath our mingled bodies a muffled sound came to us from the joyful city: a constant gasping, unendurable punctuation transmitted all the way to our maquis. And I remember the disorder we inflicted on everything around us; I remember the brightness of the sky, the darkness inside our flying cabin. It was hot, very hot, on that June 24. It seemed to us, my love, that something was about to begin that night, that our torchlit parade would set fire to the colonial night, fill with dawn the great valley of the conquest where we'd seen the light of day, where on this summer night we'd reinvented love and, in the tremors and the tricks of pleasure, conceived a dazzling event that is loath to come into being. But tonight I am depopulated: my streets are empty, desolate. All these joyous people are abandoning me.

The important persons I yearned for are breaking away from the future. The plot is being resolved at the same time that my sentence is dislocated without any fuss.

I won't accept that what was being made ready on that particular June 24 won't come about. An apocryphal sacrament joins us inextricably to the revolution. The project we've started we shall finish. To the very end I'll be the person I began to be with you, in you. These things happen. Wait for me.

I FLOOR THE gas pedal. There's a quiet place I know near the Château de Coppet. I can get there in a few minutes. I've already wasted too much time. As soon as I've finished with my passenger, I'll leave the Opel near the Coppet station and take the omnibus-train to Geneva where I'll get my Volvo back; this time, I'll take the expressway so I'll be on the terrace of the Hôtel d'Angleterre at half-past six to join K. Better yet, I'll take the train to Lausanne, I'll get a taxi at the station, and I'll be at the Hôtel d'Angleterre three or four minutes later. I'll abandon the Volvo immediately and gladly and report the incident to the Bureau, a mere formality. After all, I'm not going to travel around in a car that's already been identified. Here I am at Coppet, ravenously hungry (it's already past twelve-thirty), but I'll eat when it's over. I'm anxious to be done with H. de Heutz and all the rest. Before I board the train that will take me to Lausanne, I'm sure I'll have a few minutes to munch a *croûte zurichoise* at the station restaurant, washed down with white wine from the Valais. While I wait and as I make my way through Coppet en route to the Château, I concentrate on the problem of von Ryndt–de Heutz. The minute the trunk is open, I'll bring him out at gunpoint and haul him into the forest. It won't be hard to find the clearing where I picnicked with K one beautiful Sunday afternoon. Here is

Necker's chateau already, with its worn-out romanticism and its princely iron gate. Now I just have to turn left. Yes, that's it. I stay in second gear. All around me there's nothing and no one. I'm perplexed. This bit of road doesn't lead to the little forest, at least I don't think it does. I stop the car, letting the engine idle. I decide to go on. I advance a few hundred feet: already the broader landscape looks familiar. Yes, I'm here. I advance cautiously, nearly at a walk; if I take anyone by surprise I can always claim I'm a tourist exploring the area around the chateau. All that's missing is an edition of Benjamin Constant's diary. I know where I am now. The edge of the forest. Will I have trouble finding the entrance we used in the parchment-green Renault we'd rented for nine days? I still can hear the melody of "Desafinado." It's following me, a lyrical germ of my state of mind and of my desire to escape by hiding in this woods near the Château de Coppet, and in the piece of writing that is taking me back to Switzerland and helping me get over my hunger while I drive my passenger into the forest, brushing against the branches of the Jurassic pines that fill this woods where other exiles have ventured before me.

I turn off the ignition. A religious silence surrounds the little blue car. The air feels good, very mild. The only sound is the peaceful murmur of nature. Nothing suspicious. I take the gun from the waistband of my trousers; I turn the cylinder, check the safety, the trigger, the number of cartridges. Everything's in order. Still nothing around. I can make out the hum of a train in the distance: most likely it's the fast train between Zurich and Geneva that departs the Lausanne station at 11:56. I study the ground around the car: no trap, no unexpected difference in level, and, all things considered, enough clear space to give me room to play with my favourite banker. Now is the time. Not a sound from inside the trunk; I press my ear against its sun-warmed wall and hear absolutely nothing: it's as if I've transported a corpse. Really, there's no sign of life in the little overheated coffin. But surely H. de Heutz hasn't disappeared by magic. This is getting on my nerves. I lift the licence plate that acts as a double panel and insert the key to unlock the trunk.

Ever since I got up this morning I've been fighting a constantly renewed emotion. It's Sunday. A beautiful day. And on highway 8 between Pointe-au-Chêne and Montebello, I see a beige car travelling without me. There's something thrilling about the countryside as you leave Pointe-au-Chêne to go up the Ottawa River towards Montebello and arrive at Papineauville. I like that winding road, the lazy twists and turns of the Ottawa, the elegant hillsides along our border – secret undulations stamped with intimacy and a thousand memories of happiness. I also like this extreme landscape where there is still room for me. When all this is over, I'll settle there in a house set back from the road, not on the shore of the Ottawa but in the hinterland with its lakes and forests on the road between Papineauville and La Nation. That's where I'll buy a house, close to La Nation, near the entrance to the big estate on Lac Simon where you can portage all the way to Lac des Mauves and La Minerve. And I'll cry because it's taken me so long to find the house between Portage-de-la-Nation and La Nation or between La Nation and Ripon or on the Chénéville road between La Nation and Lac Simon. I'm terribly afraid I'll die hanging from the bars in a penitentiary cell with no time to return to La Nation, lacking the freedom to go there and stretch out in the warm summer grass, to run along the edge of the great forests filled with deer, to gaze at the enormous sky above the house where one day I'll live a sweet life without tears. Where is the country that resembles you, my true and secret native land, the country where I want to love you, where I want to die? This morning, a Sunday flooded with childlike tears, I cry like you, my child, because I've not yet arrived at the sunny fields of the countryside around La Nation that spreads out in the warm light of the country we've come back to. The next hours will break me. A few more hours would give me time to get on highway 8 at Saint-Eustache, where our brothers died, then go up the Ottawa through Oka, Saint-Placide, Carillon, Calumet and Pointe-au-Chêne, and from Pointe-au-Chêne to Montebello and on to Papineauville, where I'll head for La Nation by way of Portage-de-la-Nation and Saint-André-Avelin. A few hours would bring me to La Nation, near a house set back from history which I'll buy one day. Will I be there a few years from now? Let me go back to that summer Sunday deep in the countryside I love. Let me lie down again on the warm earth of the country, my love, and in the vulnerable bed that awaits us. The sun lights up a house that I don't know, that I won't be able to get to before night, not tomorrow or the day after or any other day before my appearance at the courthouse before the Court of Queen's Bench, where I'll have to answer for the gloom that postponed my journey to La Nation, to that house of sun and sweetness where we'll live one day. Before the judge, I'll have to answer for the night and exonerate myself of the suicidal eclipse of an entire people; I'll have to answer for my brothers who took their own lives after the defeat at Saint-Eustache and for those who imitate them, while a screen of melancholy prevents them from seeing the sun that's lighting up La Nation at this very moment. I can't break the hoops that are tightening around me and go on to the house that awaits us on the winding road from Papineauville to La Nation, to make my way towards you, my love, and towards the few days of love I still dream of living. But how am I to get out of this situation? It's impossible.

And how can I get rid of H. de Heutz? The lid of the trunk springs open a crack. I jump back. My passenger, who's curled up inside, is well and truly alive. He looks all around him, then unfolds himself suspiciously. He's obviously numb. Now he's standing here outside the trunk.

"Don't move or I'll shoot."

Now he is looking at me. He's as solemn as a Buddha minus the smile. I could shatter that image as I grip the 45 firmly in my right hand.

"And now, toss me your papers."

He complies. I bend down to pick up his Florentine leather wallet. Three blue-on-blue hundred-Swiss-franc notes. A business card: Charles-André Junker, Imefbank, rue Petitot 6, Geneva. Telephone: 26 12 70. That's a banker I'll soon be consulting about the appreciation of our revolutionary investments in Switzerland. Mechanically I pocket the engraved card and the 100 FS notes. Quickly I empty the compartment of his papers. There's a driver's licence in the name of François-Marc de Saugy, boulevard des Philosophes 16, Liège. Profession: procurator.

"Procurator of Carl von Ryndt and H. de Heutz I assume?"

"I don't know what you're talking about. I don't know those names . . ."

"It's pointless to waste my time, Monsieur . . . de Saudy . . ."

"De Saugy . . ."

". . . Monsieur de Saugy. Your ID is in order: you have an expert supplier, I can see that. But I'm not interested in the forger's art . . . I know who you are – de Heutz or von Ryndt, I don't care! – and I know that you're working against us. I may as well tell you, we've dismantled your clever organization and we're well aware of your close ties with your counterparts in Montreal and Ottawa. To put it bluntly, you've had it. Now that we're face to face again, you'll understand my dilemma: it's you or me. It's the logic of battle. And since I'm the one who is holding you, my dear banker, your time is up. You can say your prayers, as long as they're brief . . ."

I see him decompose before my eyes. No doubt he's trying to get out of this and reverse the situation. This time, though, I'm the one holding the weapon and I'm very comfortable in this position. If I feel relaxed, it's simply because I've got the upper hand. In a way I'm savouring my advantage.

"Look . . . Please. Let me explain . . ."

". . . explain how you collaborate with the RCMP and its big sister the CIA; and how you regularly contravene article 47b of the Swiss federal constitution to gain access to the bank accounts of certain anonymous investors. Sure, go ahead and explain. I'm all ears."

"I don't know what you're talking about, Monsieur. Believe me, the truth is sadder and certainly less mysterious. At the chateau this morning I put on a show for you. I played my part . . . I repeat: the truth is rather depressing. What can I tell you? I'm seriously ill. For weeks now I've been living like a fugitive . . ."

"Don't tire yourself. I know you're going to talk nonsense to try to gain some time. But it's not working."

"I'm not making this up, I swear. It's the truth. I swear, on the heads of my children! . . . Yes, I have two children, two little boys. And I haven't seen them for weeks. They're in Belgium. I abandoned them. I ran away. Couldn't face up to my problems any more. It was the bankruptcy: I didn't know what to do. And I panicked. One night I wrote a letter to my wife, confessing everything, then I took off without seeing her again, like a coward. My wife didn't have enough to live on for a week. I boarded the express train to Basel. And I thought that once I was there, where no one knows me, I could steal some money and send it to my wife . . ."

Listening to his story I feel giddy. H. de Heutz seems so overwhelmed and genuinely moved that I let down my guard. Yet it's obvious that he's having a joke at my expense. This entire cock-and-bull story bears a strange resemblance to the one I told him this morning at the Château d'Echandens when I was unilaterally disarming him. Right now H. de Heutz is spinning exactly the same convoluted yarn. It's plagiarism. Does he really think I'll swallow it?

"I'm not lying. I went to Basel first. I thought that with my Mauser, I'd work miracles and become a high-class thief overnight: impeccable, polite with cashiers, unpunished to the end. I thought all I'd need was this weapon and my despair, and in a few days I'd make my fortune and send money orders to my wife. I lived in that state for a few days but I never stole anything, never sent a penny to my wife. Every day I'd think: 'Today's the day. Today, I'll succeed.' And I'd tell myself that soon, when I was rich, I'd bring my wife and children to Switzerland. We could settle here happily, rent a villa in the mountains in the Val d'Hérens near Evolène. I know a wonderful spot around there. I want to live there with my wife and children. You can't imagine how I long to see those boys. I don't even know if my wife's been able to get her hands on any money. When I left Liège I had debts, a mass of debts she didn't know about. Could she have grown discouraged and killed herself, after strangling the children? I'm afraid. I don't know what to do. I wonder if I'll ever see my two little boys again. They probably expect me to turn up at dinner-time every evening. When I was in Liège, I always came home from the office at the same time. They must be asking their mother when I'll be back, and she must be telling them that I've gone away for my work or that I'm dead. It would be good, actually, if she told them I'd died in the war and that I would never come back to play with them . . ."

"Do you think I'm an idiot, Monsieur de Heutz? Do you think you can distract me with that fairy tale? And on top of everything else you've got the gall to serve me up the same story I told you this morning . . . Really, you're piling it on a little too thick for my liking, to say nothing of the fact that you've got absolutely no imagination!"

As I say that, he bursts out sobbing with such sincerity that it's unsettling. H. de Heutz really is crying like a sorrowing father, like a man who's overwhelmed by pain and doesn't have the strength to face up to life. But I keep reminding myself that this pathetic individual is recounting a soap opera for the sole purpose of escaping (but how?) from the trap where I'm holding him. My job is to stay alert in this preposterous competition and to remember that only one design underlies his performance: to divert my attention, dull my reflexes, instill just enough doubt in me to make me relax my vigilance for as little as a fraction of a second, and to take advantage of it. I constantly have to refute my distress at the sight of him so despondent, his face distraught with emotion and bathed in tears. The man is an impostor: F.M. de Saugy, von Ryndt, H. de Heutz: they're one and the same person. H. de Heutz is an enemy I've brought here for just one reason: to shoot him in cold blood. Nothing in the world must divert me from my plan. Nothing! Particularly not this parade of emotions being put on by our Africanist. In all sincerity, I acknowledge that H. de Heutz is a consummate artist. He has a diabolical gift for falsifying what is plausible; if I weren't on guard, he'd have roped me in, maybe even convinced me that he's my brother, that we were destined to meet and understand each other. Really, I'm dealing with the devil.

"All right. This performance has gone on long enough. Don't wear yourself out over nothing. I don't believe one word you've told me . . ."

"I have no reason to make anything up. I know that it's over for me and that in a few seconds – at the time you've chosen – you'll kill me like a dog. I don't want to live in any case, I haven't got the strength . . ."

And with that he starts to cry again desperately. Though I consider him to be the last of the liars, a contemptible tool of the counter-revolution, I have to acknowledge that he really is crying; I can see it.

"I'll never see my children again; I don't want to, I don't deserve to . . . The last time I was with them, I cried. That's the image they have of their father. I was distraught. I'd lost my job but I hadn't told anyone yet. I couldn't even tell my wife. I'd already started hanging around the banks, waiting for I don't know what – a miracle maybe. And I'd begun to follow people in the street, imagining that at some point the opportunity would present itself to strike them down and grab their wallets stuffed with money. I thought about nothing else, but when the time came to act, I was numb. Kill me! It's the best thing that could happen to me. I beg you. Shoot me. For pity's sake . . ."

My finger is on the trigger: I just have to press it and I'll grant his wish. Yet I hesitate. The story he persists in telling presents me with a dilemma. Why has he chosen to tell me exactly the same unlikely tale I served up to him this morning when he had me in his sights in the grand salon of the Château d'Echandens? His very boldness fascinates me and, who knows, makes him nearly likeable. When he started his spiel, he already knew that I wouldn't fall into such a crude trap. He must have foreseen that I wouldn't be taken in by this invention of his. If that's so, if he has embellished the scheme that I myself worked out this morning, it's not by accident or through a chance combination due to the simple laws of probability. H. de Heutz was following a precise plan. He had something in mind when he dragged me into this heap of improbability and irony. What was it? Maybe he wanted to pass on a coded message. But no, that's nonsense, because between H. de Heutz and me there could be no cipher, no code, no reason whatsoever to exchange any message. There is only a relentless break and the impossibility of communicating in any other way than with gunfire. If I'm probing his deepest intentions, maybe I'm about to fall into the trap he's set for me and I'm reacting exactly as he wanted. My very fascination, as well as its corollary, methodical doubt and hesitation, is something he knowingly provoked. But why?

"Don't move or I'll shoot . . ."

He's still crying. This is getting on my nerves. I don't know what to do. It's hard to look at him and listen to him. It turns

me inside out. What's most puzzling is his incredible auto-
biography, which he's invented not in order to fool me but for
some more perverse reason: to captivate me, cause me to doubt
the reason of state that's confronting us here in this confined
space, conditioning me to see this man who's speaking in bad
faith as an enemy to kill. Who is he anyway, this weeping individual? Is he Carl von Ryndt, with a cover as a banker but
mainly an enemy agent; or is he H. de Heutz, Walloon specialist
in Scipio Africanus and in counter-revolution; or could he be
the third man, François-Marc de Saugy by name, who's in the
grip of a nervous breakdown and an acute attack of dissocia-
tion? When all's said and done, I'm probably losing my way
in the impenetrable trap of this dark trinity as I equivocate over
the genuine presence of a threefold enemy and over the highly
pathological etiology of a man standing a few steps from me,
plunged in a depiction of pain that's no more genuine than the
very name he uses. To tell the truth, H. de Heutz's power cap-
tivates me even more than it terrifies me. Who am I actually
dealing with? The transmigrated shadow of Ferragus? This
unknown man attracts me at the very moment when I'm
preparing to kill him. The mystery about him confounds my
meditation and I stand before him gasping, unable to direct
my thoughts at another object or to combat the morbid
attraction he exerts over me.

Everything slows down. My very heartbeats seem more
widely spaced. The supersonic agility of my mind collapses
suddenly under the malevolent charm of H. de Heutz. I stand
motionless, transformed into a pillar of salt, and I can't help
seeing myself as thunderstruck. A sovereign event is occur-
ring right now as I occupy a tiny space in a charming woods
that looks down on Coppet, while the time that separates me
from my appointment with K on the terrace of the Hôtel
d'Angleterre keeps shrinking. In the presence of this man
who's impossible to identify, I seem to be still seeking the
pure reason that's made me pursue him so desperately, that

should incline me to pull the trigger of the Mauser and fire at him to break the troubling relationship that has sprung up between us. I keep looking at him, I hear his sobs, and a kind of mystery fills me with sacred indecision. An event I've stopped controlling is unfurling solemnly within me, sending me into a deep trance.

LESS VERBAL now, my sorrow is running secretly in my veins. The haunting music of "Desafinado" drives away the sun. I watch it go down, flaming, in the middle of Lac Léman, its posthumous light setting fire to the clay strata of the Pre-Alps. A city seven times buried, its written memory is no longer touched by the generative flame of revolution. Delinquent inspiration is drowned in the cuttlefish ink that causes the lake to shudder in front of Coppet.

Nothing is free here: neither my compulsion, nor the greasy traction of ink on the realm of fancy, nor the movements sensed by H. de Heutz, nor the freedom that has devolved upon me to kill him when the time is right. Nothing is free here, nothing: not even this impetuous escape that I'm manipulating with my fingertips and think I'm controlling, when in fact it is obliterating me. Nothing! Not even the plot, nor the order in which my memories light up, nor the entombment of my nights of love, nor the Galilean swaying of my women. Something tells me that an earlier model is transforming my improvisation into some atavistic form, that an ancient alluvium is embracing the instant river that escapes me. I'm not writing, I am written. The future act has long since known me. The uncreated novel is dictated to me word by word and I appropriate it as I go, following the Geneva convention on literary copyright. I am creating something that outdistances me, that sets down before me the mark of my unpredictable footprints. The imagination is a scar. I live my own invention and what I kill is already dead. The images I imprint on my retina were already there. I do not invent. What awaits H. de Heutz in the romantic woods surrounding the Château de Coppet will be communicated to me soon, when my hand, busy speeding up history, is launched into action by some words that will come before me. Everything is waiting for me. Everything precedes me with a precision that I unveil even as I move to get closer to it. Though I'm running now, it's as if my anterior past has laid down my approach and uttered the words I think I'm imagining.

For a long time I dreamed of devising my own movement and rhythm, of laying down with my own fervent strides the road to follow. Yes, during all those years I dreamed of a triumphant rush I would produce second by second. But I can lay down nothing but words, struck in advance in the image of the absolute woman I encountered somewhere between Acton Vale and Tingwick, which is now called Chénier, between a certain June 24 and my eternal motile night. Every fragment of this unfinished novel reminds me of that fragment of road in the Eastern Townships, of a fragment of night torn from a *fête nationale*. This hybrid novel is merely a disorderly variation on other books by unknown writers. Mired in a bed of clay, I follow the course, I never invent. That holds true for everything I write: here I am, deep in an impasse where I no longer want to move forward. That depressing observation ought to let me break free of it and find a countertruth to make up for it. But I can find nothing beyond my evidence, especially because I resist transposing it into a rigid system. I reject any systematization that would plunge me deeper still into the agony of something not yet created. The pseudo-creative novelist merely draws his characters' gestures and relationships directly from an old repertoire. If I denounce as futile any attempt at originality, perhaps I must continue within that pitiful darkness and burrow within this darkened labyrinth. No negotiable depravity can shield me from the sharp despair I experience at the thought of all the variables that can enter into the composition of an original work. But why am I so concerned about this question of absolute originality? I don't know. But ever since my mind has stopped trying to solve this riddle, I've been afflicted with a progressive slowdown, struck by a growing paralysis. My hand no longer moves forward. I'm reluctant to do anything more; suddenly I don't even know how to behave. I have a powerful sense that the next turn will be dangerous and that I risk everything when I admit why I'm hesitating. It's no longer the operative originality of literature I render harmless, it's the individual's existence that suddenly bursts and disenchants me! But if this shock that's annihilating my ambition to write something in an original way is so devastating, if I'm suddenly deprived of my reason for writing because I perceive my forthcoming book as predicted and marked in advance, according to the Dewey system, with an infinitesimal coefficient of individuation, and because at the same time I still want to write, it means that writing doesn't become pointless simply because I am stripping it of its need to be original, or because this genetic function doesn't define it. At least an urge to be original isn't the only thing that improves the image of the literary endeavour. One can undertake to write a spy novel that's set anomalously on the shores of Lac Léman with some other motive than creating a unique work! Originality at all costs is a chivalrous ideal, an aesthetic Holy Grail that falsifies any expedition. Jerusalem the second, that overdone singularity, is nothing but a crusader's obsession, a mythical retransposition of a stroke of fortune that is the basis on which powerful capitalism has been erected.

I see in this novel I'm writing, in this daily book that's beginning to give me more pleasure, a meaning different from the powerful novelty of its final format. I follow this book from hour to hour and from day to day, and I'm no more likely to give up on it than I am to commit suicide. This broken book resembles me. This mass of paper is a product of history, an unfinished fragment of my own essence and thus an impure testimony to the faltering revolution I continue to express in my own way through my institutionalized delirium. This book is cursory and uncertain, as I am, and its true meaning cannot be dissociated from the date of its composition or from events that have happened within a given period of time between my native country and my exile, between a certain July 26 and a June 24. Written by a prisoner held ransom at ten thousand guineas for a detox cure, this book is the bitter fruit of an anecdotal incident that sent me from a prison to a clinic, that obliges me to be methodically busy for days and days so I won't grow discouraged. This book is the tirelessly repeated act of a patriot who's waiting in the timeless void for the chance to take up arms again. Moreover, it embraces the very shape of the time to come: in it and through it I am exploring my indecision and my unlikely future. Overall, it points to a conclusion that it won't contain because it will follow the full stop that I'll set at the bottom of my last page. I no longer insist on pursuing the spectre of originality, something that would actually keep me inside the nitrogenous sphere of inflationary art. The anticipated masterpiece isn't my business. My dream is of a totalitarian art in constant genesis. The one form I've been pursuing, confusedly, since I began this work is the formless one assumed by my imprisoned existence: an impulse constantly broken by the fragmented timetable of seclusion, a binary oscillation between hypostasis and aggression. Here my every move is an attempt to deny my isolation; I seek untidily any earlier existences where I was not a prisoner, but was flung in every direction like a corrupted missile. From that contradiction no doubt come the wild fluctuations in what I write, a frenzied alternation of drownings and resurfacings. Whenever I come back to this paper a new episode is born. Every writing session creates a pure event, attached to a novel only to the degree, unreadable but terrifying, to which I myself am connected to my broken-down existence. A naked event, my book is writing me, it is open to understanding only on condition that it's not removed from its historical context. And here I am, suddenly dreaming that my epic, which is losing its sense of reality, is inscribed on the national calendar of a people without history! How ridiculous, how pitiful! It's true that we have no history. And we'll start having one only at that uncertain moment when the revolutionary war begins. Our history will be launched in the blood of a revolution that is breaking me, that I've served poorly: on that day, with slashed veins, we'll make our debut in the world. On that day, a bloody intrigue will build on our quicksand an eternal pyramid that will let us measure the size of our dead trees. History will begin to write itself when we give to our pain the rhythm and the blinding power of war. Everything will take on the flamboyant colours of history when we march into battle, machine-guns at the ready. When our brothers die in ambushes, leaving the women alone to celebrate June 24, our writing will no longer be an event, it will become a document. The act alone will prevail. Only the guerrilla's elusive and deadly action will be seen as historical; only despair that has led to action will be recognized as revolutionary. Any other writing, any other song, will be assigned to the pre-revolutionary period.

The revolution will come the way love came to us one June 24 when, naked and glorious, we annihilated each other on a bed of shadow while a conquered people was learning how to march in step. It will come in the manner of the absolute and repeated event that consumed us, whose plenitude is haunting me tonight. This nameless book is undecided, as I myself have been since the Seven Years War, anarchical too as one must be at the dawn of a revolution. We can't wish soberly for revolution, we can't explain it like a syllogism or call it in the way that we proceed in court. The inevitable disorder is already gaining on me, moulding my soul: I am invaded like the field of a battle I prepare for feverishly. It is on us and in us that the great disruption begins; it is in our vulnerable existences and our loving encounters that the first blows are dealt. The anarchy that heralds its approach manifests itself through our ministry; it throws us in prison, broken, unsatisfied, sick. The revolution I call for has wounded me. Before hostilities have begun, my own battle is already over. Prematurely disqualified, evacuated to the interior, out of the line of fire, I'm a wounded soldier; but what a cruel wound, for according to the letter there's no war yet and that's what is wounding me. My country is injuring me. Its prolonged failure has flung me to the ground. Wounded and ghostly, I experience behind bars the first tremors of a story that has never been told, that resembles this book only because it too is untold and because I don't know the names of my brothers who will be killed in battle, any more than I know the titles of the different chapters of my novel. I don't even know what will become of my characters who are waiting for me in the Coppet woods. I've reached the point of wondering if I'll get to the Hôtel d'Angleterre in time, because that's the only thing that concerns me now: the time that separates me from our meeting is slipping by.

Melancholy permeates me through all the valves of reading and boredom. Between the second-last sentence and this one, I've let four or five national revolutions pass, the same number of empires, of holy alliances and joyous entries. In the same rift I've seen a dozen revolutions turn to failure, starting with the revolution of Geneva in 1781, that of the United Provinces of the Netherlands in 1787, that of the Austrian Netherlands, and of Liège. In less than twenty-four hours I lived from 1776 to 1870, from the Boston Tea Party to the Camp de la Misère on the Meuse near Sedan, seeking nourishment in the harsh water of my memories. Since yesterday, somewhere between H. de Heutz and Toussaint l'Ouverture, I've been submerged in the secular water of revolution. I have shuddered at the thousand suicides of Tchernychevski and at the insurrectional romanticism of Mazzini. These elder brothers in despair and outrage are nearly as present in me as the Patriotes, my unknown brothers, who wait for me secretly, impatiently. Will they recognize me?

My brothers-in-war are virtual, as are the unlikely characters who await me further along in this story, who may surprise me, and as I encourage them to do specific deeds, they'll oblige me to remember them, not wait for them as I'm doing now, fascinated by the area of freedom they move in as if they were inside a prehistory I have to end by writing something that they haven't done yet, that they'll do in the exact proportion to which my indifferent invention brings them up to date.

All night long the centuries file past beneath the windows of our love. But I've lost you, my love, and this music no longer intoxicates me. I must see you again. Without you, I die. The vast landscape of our love is darkening. I see neither the ravaged pedestal of the High Alps nor the great dead flows of the glaciers. I see nothing: neither the synclinal vault of the lake nor the overturned mass of the Hôtel d'Angleterre nor the Château d'Ouchy nor the crest of the grand hotels of Lausanne nor the invisible chalet I've dreamed of buying in Evolène in the high valley of Hérens, nor the vesperal form of the Château de Coppet. Nothing can save me now. My leaded coffin is sinking to the bottom of an uninhabited lake. Decades of failures and pitched battles no longer sustain me, any more than the centuries of my life in love that have been reduced to a few dates on an envelope.

I need you; I need to retrieve the thread of our story and the ellipsis that will take me back to the heat of our two consumed bodies. I don't know where to pick up. I remember that dialogue with H. de Heutz in the Coppet woods. But so much has happened since then, at such a brisk pace, and I'm so engaged in this jolting process that it's less urgent for me to recount what happened between Coppet and now than to concentrate on what is happening and what is threatening to happen. Time sweeps me along. This long wait has in no way conditioned me for action. And when there is action, I'm caught off guard, compelled to improvise even though I'd carefully prepared myself for any eventuality. All that I should have guessed when I found myself in the Château d'Echandens, facing H. de Heutz who had me in his sights.

IN FACT, THINGS started to blur at the point in that confused meeting where I was acting, while admitting implicitly that there could be no witnesses to my conversation with H. de Heutz. I got out of the trap, and it didn't occur to me that, while I was pushing H. de Heutz ahead of me at gunpoint, some other person was very close by, observing me, no doubt delighted to watch me bash down a wide-open door with such bravado. It was during the interval between my confinement and my flight, between the time when I disarmed H. de Heutz and when I stuffed him into the Opel's trunk, that I stopped being logical. I was behaving like a fugitive who couldn't be punished while I jumped with both feet into a gaping trap. Moreover, I was displaying a deranged self-confidence. Yes, I should have been careful, because everything happened as it does in the movies with murky ease. The more I think back to those few minutes, the more I wonder how plausible this sequence is. I even wonder if H. de Heutz didn't politely slow down his reaction time when I went to disarm him simply to help me out. I'm sure he did: he cheated imperceptibly to give me time to get into the victor's skin, to smoothly abide by the scenario that had been devised to trap me. H. de Heutz didn't resist my injunction. He curled up in the trunk of the car. Just as I was slamming the lid on his head, he must have given a hint of a contented smile, for I was meekly obeying him and he didn't even have to state his orders clearly. I had become his medium: unbeknownst to me, H. de Heutz had driven me into a cataleptic state and, from his hermetically sealed position, he continued to guide me into recklessness and rapture. If only I'd had the strength to turn around, I'd have spotted two eyes fixed on me at one of the windows on the north side of the chateau.

It's possible that the situation I'm in now is making me over-state the degree of premeditation behind the trap H. de Heutz, dear man, had set for me. Let's admit that he'd anticipated my getaway attempt and that, among other possibilities, I might jump into the little Opel to do it. All right. But how could he have precisely imagined I'd make him get into the trunk of the car I was borrowing from him? He couldn't foresee what approach I would make, so he was predicting something else: that I'd commandeer the Opel for my getaway! Following the internal logic of this method, after H. de Heutz had rearmed he'd have taken off after me in the other car, which I hadn't seen but which had to have been in the garage, whose doors were shut. What's more, H. de Heutz was positive he'd catch up with me: there's just one road through Echandens and as soon as he saw me drive away in one direction or the other, he had plenty of time to calmly open the garage doors and take out the other car. In any event, I was bound to be driving down his road with a few minutes' lead at most. A strictly technical problem: I couldn't escape from him – unless of course in his haste he lost control of his vehicle and smashed his skull against a hundred-year-old tree, which was highly unlikely if you know H. de Heutz.

What happened was that as soon as I departed from H. de Heutz's plan, he was neutralized and, who knows, maybe even helpless – for a few seconds anyway. Because it would be underestimating him to deny that he'd anticipated every-thing that might happen, even his own death! Consequently, the other person was already at my back, veiled by the curtains at a window. And that other person had watched me manoeuvre H. de Heutz, following a rather baroque protocol; when he saw me turn onto the road that runs through Echandens to Saint-Prex, he'd had time to pull on his jacket, secure his high-calibre weapon in an embossed leather holster, go to the garage from the inside, take out a big car and, unbeknownst to me, start tailing me, since I hadn't taken the precaution of glancing inside the garage to check the make of the car. Now, since I knew neither the make of the car that was following me nor the identity of its driver, I didn't even know if I was being escorted, because of course the other person – H. de Heutz's friend – took the precautions necessary to avoid attracting my attention, constantly changing his position on the road, his angle of surveillance, and the distance between us. At one point he must have taken the liberty of coming within a hair's breadth of the Opel and looking me in the eye just like that. The highway to Geneva is wide enough and busy enough to conceal the expert designs of a spy. When he passed, nearly touching me, how could I have known it was him? How can you unmask an enemy when, paradoxically, you've implicitly eliminated him and he doesn't exist?

And so I drove from Echandens to Place Simon-Goulart in Geneva without thinking, even as a suspicious reflex, that throughout this enchanting journey the other person was on the road very close to me, travelling along in my wake – or was I in his? – passing me on the left or right, getting a solid lead over me (while keeping my reflection in his rear-view mirror) or impetuously letting me pass while never losing sight of me. In Geneva I went directly to Place Simon-Goulart, which in the transparency of daylight opens onto an expanse of mountains and eternal snow. Just as I was parking near the Banque Arabe, an innocuous-looking stranger was parking his car near mine, never losing sight of me. It was that other person! He observed me at leisure while I was listing all the reasons why I should clear out of Place Simon-Goulart where my Volvo was waiting. He may even have taken a position behind the great barred window of the Banque Arabe, pretending to fill out a form while keeping an eye on me as I hesitated, gracelessly and awkwardly, not too sure what to do with the Opel and the Volvo – one full, the other empty – while the morning sun illuminated the great belt of peaks and spires, plunging the layered flanks of Mont Maudit into shadow. There was no doubt about it: I'd been duped from start to finish. It had all started in the grand salon of the Château d'Echandens when I was sitting across from H. de Heutz and the three big windows that looked out on the chateau's elegant grounds and the incantatory space of the great valley, where Lac Léman was lighted up by the first rays of sun which at that moment was at its apogee.

For twenty-four hours now I've hardly slept. At two a.m. I was still following a shadow that was following me, and at sunrise, around half-past five, I was facing my personal enemy number one, demoralized from listing the mistakes that had brought me to this sorry pass, unable to imagine anything to fill the conversational gaps except the story of a nervous breakdown: two children, abandoned wife, escape, my pitiful ambition to rob banks and my final resolution to make judicious use of my special Colt, blowing my brains out in a vacant lot in Carouge. Since yesterday I haven't had time to recover except during a few hours of comatose sleep. And now in a sense I'm enjoying an infinitesimal intermission which will give me just enough time to figure out what's happened to me and to prepare myself for what's ahead, an infinite margin of obstacles and time separating me from our meeting on the terrace of the Hôtel d'Angleterre. The latest events surprised me so much that I have trouble recalling the order in which they occurred. I remember H. de Heutz leaning against the trunk of the car, overcome by suffering and constantly recalling his final hours with his wife and children in Belgium, somewhere in the former Austrian Netherlands. At the last moment, he told me, he'd hesitated between suicide in the Meuse and flight. He also told me that what hurt him most was his vague recollections of his two little boys, for he couldn't clearly recall their features or the timbre of their voices. H. de Heutz wept abundantly as he described his appalling life.

And that was when I perceived a sign! Everything began to move at lightning speed; first, I ran through the Coppet woods, heading for what I assumed to be the very heart of the forest. After a few minutes of this frantic race I came to a promontory that looks down on the village of Coppet. There, in a dazzling landscape just above the turquoise water and facing the Roc d'Enfer that stands at the front of the tangled group of massifs, I pricked up my ear: no suspicious sounds, none I could make out at any rate. Groping in my back pocket, I realized that I still had the keys for the Opel. Oh well, H. de Heutz didn't need them now: he'd simply got into the other person's car. For a moment it seemed to me (but was I mistaken?) that the other person was a woman: no doubt the one who'd been walking on H. de Heutz's arm through the streets of Geneva and had suddenly disappeared as if by magic. How could I be sure? I'd only caught a glimpse of the car: I hadn't so much seen it as guessed at it. It had practically sprung up behind me, silently, on the small road. It was H. de Heutz's smile that made me sense it, his gaze that made me react, even more than the tires gliding along the asphalt and the engine's imperceptible roar. That was when I realized I was surrounded and therefore had no choice: his sudden intrusion was forcing me to execute H. de Heutz before a witness and, at worst, expose myself to a surprise shot by the intruder. I turned around, I saw the car slip behind the leaves, and I spied the other person at the wheel: a woman. I saw her blonde hair first. But could I trust such a fleeting sight taxed in advanced by such hallucinatory circumstances? The blonde hair was probably a side effect of the sun's brightness and my own dazzlement, so that I couldn't actually be sure the other person is a woman, one who improbably has blonde hair. A fleeting sight distorted by danger, what I remember is vague and uncertain, unless fear made my vision particularly keen! Anyway ... When I heard a car door slam, I quickly realized that if I tried to get away in the Opel, I'd erupt into the middle of the woman's field of vision and give her a moving target. I kept H. de Heutz in my sights while I walked around the car. Once I was in front of the grille I was in a better position. H. de Heutz was facing me, right in the middle of the historic space where the other person's silhouette would soon appear. The seconds galloped by faster than my thoughts. I came within a hair's breadth of pressing the trigger, spelling the end of H. de Heutz. But what would happen then? The other person, the blonde woman, was very close to me but I didn't know exactly where: I could only sense her. If I had rushed to kill H. de Heutz, she'd have emptied her magazine into my head and I'd have collapsed inopportunely. Before I lost my way in this brisk current of possibles and imponderables, I made a hint of a movement of retreat, on tiptoe at first, keeping my gun pointed at H. de Heutz, who was looking at me; then, after I was far enough away that my footsteps were muffled, I started running towards what I thought was the heart of the forest – only to find myself, after a few minutes of an exhausting sprint, in the natural observatory that looks down on the village of Coppet, opposite the gutted temple of the Dents du Midi, alone at last, absolutely alone, not yet knowing if I was threatened or unpunished, but well aware that H. de Heutz was no longer within range of my gun and that though I'd narrowly escaped a second trap, I had failed doubly in my mission. H. de Heutz was still alive. And the deadline for my meeting with K, closer now, was haunting me.

One o'clock sounded at the Coppet town hall. In spite of everything, a tremendous sense of well-being flooded me and

I filled my lungs with the cool air that a light breeze was wafting towards the vineyards in the back country. All around me a deep calm prevailed. The hazy high noon suggested sweetness and rest. A thin light bathed the valley of the Rhône and the raging architecture of the landscape that unfolds around Coppet in as many styles as there are eras, from the recent civilizations of the southern valley to the folds of high glacial antiquity. Stationed on this promontory, able to take in at a single glance the turbulent opening that, from the Furka to Viège, from Viège to Martigny by way of the steep corridor of the Haut-Valais, has impetuously carved the slopes, the ridges, and the granite walls that are constantly hacked to pieces on the heights, tangled in a calcareous embrace from the Haut de Cry to the Dent de Morcles, I gazed out at the incomparable script of this anonymous masterpiece that was written in the debris of avalanches, of morainal streaks and poorly carved splinters of an implacable genesis. I took a long look at this interrupted landscape that extends in a flared cirque from the foothills of the Bernese Alps to the glorious peaks of the Valais massifs and the Pennine Alps. Then I took a few steps on the promontory and sprinted down a small path that brought me to Coppet, to a small square bounded on the south by the awe-inspiring passage of the Rhône and that, imperceptible, of floating mountains. Around this tiny square, shops displayed themselves to the passerby. My appetite restored by the sight of the window of a fancy-food shop, I decided to treat myself to a good lunch. The clock on the town hall showed ten past one. In just a few minutes I was on the Grand-Rue heading for the centre of Coppet.

I stopped at the Auberge des Émigrés whose back gave onto the lake, its front on the Grand-Rue. I took a table for two by the window so that I was facing against the current of the Rhône and into the alluvial chasm set into its walls of spires and crystalline massifs. Delighted to be sitting down after so many hours of hunting and being hunted, I suddenly felt free of any worry about H. de Heutz. I'll have plenty of time to think effectively, I mused, when I have something in my stomach. First I ordered crêpes stuffed with ham and Emmenthal and a bottle of Réserve du Vidôme. Things were going well. The Auberge des Émigrés is a very pleasant place; I was practically alone. A couple at the back were speaking English. The fruity taste of the white wine from the hills of Yvorne finally convinced me that I'd been right to come to this restaurant; anyway, I had to eat, because I wouldn't have been able to keep up the frightening tempo of this race with the hagiographer of Scipio Africanus much longer. Forgetting for a moment that the appearance seemingly by magic of a blonde woman at the wheel of a car had kept me from finishing off H. de Heutz, I tucked into the crêpes hungrily, stopping now and then for a sip of the well-chosen fruity white wine. I'd get my wits back after a good meal. And it was delicious! After the crêpes came sautéed chicken from Mont Noir in a thick sauce, with a fine vintage Château Puidoux. With no pressure of time, I succumbed to the pleasure of eating and drinking and to the no less intoxicating one of being on a balcony above the lake in this ancient landscape, where I was happy to stop and peer out at its smallest folds. Over more than forty-eight hours I'd lost my way a thousand times in this collage of mountains and an awe-inspiring valley, never breaking away from it. Only the axis had changed since the moment when I spotted the woman I love near Place de la Riponne.

And it was that same motionless lake, spied the next day at dawn, that flowed in us after a twelve-month separation, and that we returned to yesterday when we emerged from our caress at the hour when the sun slants towards the Dent du Chat and the Grand Chartreuse. In two days of slow travel from Place de la Riponne to the Hôtel d'Angleterre, from the Château d'Ouchy to the Tour de Peilz, from Clarens to Yvorne and Aigle, from Aigle to Château d'Oex by way of the Col des

Mosses, from Château d'Oex to Carouge, and then from Echandens to Geneva and Geneva to Coppet, I have only circumscribed the same inverted vault, thereby circling the great river bed that enthralls me even now as I abandon myself to the effusive course of words . . .

WHEN I TURNED my attention to the cheese, a Tomme de Savoie and a small portion of Vacherin, washed down with a Côtes du Rhône, it was already a quarter to two, and nearly five past when I tossed back a Williamine to revive myself before leaving this memorable restaurant. Outside on Coppet's Grand-Rue, all was calm. A good tourist, I took a few steps along the sidewalk. Released from all obsessions and immunized against a certain H. de Heutz by the wines and the Williamine, I savoured the pure pleasure of ambling along as I liked to do in Leysin every morning, strolling to Trumpier to buy the Lausanne *Gazette*, then climbing up to the cog-railway station, where I could lean on the balustrade and gaze out at the network of the great Alps from the Pic Chaussy as far as the Grand Muveran and then, in the background just in front of me, the Tour Noir, the Chardonnets, the Aiguille du Druz and the Dents du Midi, and, on my right in a chain running south, the Crête de Linges, the Cornettes de Bise, the Jumelles and a sort of hazy screen whose condensation indicated Lac Léman. That same deformed cordillera still surrounded me when I was idling around Coppet's Grand-Rue, carefree and happy.

I stopped to look at a bookstore window: there was a photo of Charles-Ferdinand Ramuz, surrounded by copies of

Derborence and *La Beauté sur la Terre*. Out of curiosity, and probably because I wanted to postpone the moment when I'd have nothing to do but think about H. de Heutz, I stepped inside. The interior of the shop gave an impression of serenity. Books covered the walls: clearly organized and arranged by collection, they formed geometric spots of various colours and sizes. I was careful to let the bookseller know that I wasn't looking for anything specific, and he kindly urged me to browse to my heart's content. First, I took down the *Blue Guide* to Switzerland and opened it to Coppet. I expected to find a small-scale map of the town that would help me locate my position and that of the Opel, which was still at the edge of the woods, and also to reconstitute the route I'd taken through the little forest to the promontory. There was nothing of the sort though, only a host of information about the families of Necker and Madame de Staël, who'd been placed under surveillance in her own chateau. I replaced the *Guide* as if I'd changed my mind about doing more travelling in Switzerland. Aware that time was passing and that I seemed unaware of it, I wasn't really interested in the titles that paraded past my eyes. Suddenly, I spoke to the bookseller:

"Excuse me, Monsieur . . . I'm looking for a historical work on Caesar and the Helvetians by a writer called H. de Heutz . . ."

"H. de Heutz . . . that sounds familiar."

The bookseller began to search his shelves, systematic and diligent.

"Do you know who published it?"

"Sorry, I don't."

"The name Heutz does ring a bell . . ."

It was already half-past two when I resolved what my next move would be. I put my hand in my pocket, pretended I was combing through the history books, and counted my keys without showing them. I'd made my decision. Then, noting that the bookseller was having more trouble than I was to locate something by H. de Heutz, I thanked him for his efforts. Out of courtesy, I picked up the first book that came to hand, Greene's *Our Man in Havana*, and paid for it, already anxious to get outside and swing into action. On the sidewalk of the Grande-Rue, I looked in vain for a taxi. Then I set out resolutely towards the station. Before I even got there, I hailed a taxi, which stopped.

"To the chateau!"

Giving that order let me regain full possession of my strength. Slumped on the seat, I was thinking with salutary certainty that I was on my way to a positive result, at one masterstroke getting rid of H. de Heutz and then, free as the breeze, joining K on the terrace of the Hôtel d'Angleterre. A few minutes later the taxi stopped at the gate to the Necker estate. To allow the driver time to turn around and head back towards the village, I pretended to be studying the decrepit front of the chateau and the wrought-iron gate that kept people out. As soon as I could no longer see the taxi, I started walking like a solitary stroller along the narrow road that turns sharply to follow the edge of the forest. There was no one around. The rustling of leaves, the song of the birds and of the wind from the moraine filled the pastoral silence of nature. Then the small blue shape of the Opel came into sight through a clump of trees. I stopped briefly, alert for any strange rustling that would warn of an enemy presence. But there were no false notes in the smooth murmur of this beautiful summer day. Cautiously, I took a few steps in the forest and found myself back in the place that I'd fled just a few hours earlier. The trunk of the car was still open, the door was swaying feebly in the wind. I closed it, unable to do so silently. I had no trouble spotting the proper key, which I inserted in the ignition to get the little Opel on the road.

The key chain held four keys in all: now I'd just have to try the three others in the lock of the Château d'Echandens. One of them would surely give me access to the chateau, to which I'd decided to return. A search, even a hasty one, would certainly tell me something and perhaps I'd make some discoveries that would help us unmask our enemies. Moreover, by gaining admittance to the chateau I would thwart all the expectations of H. de Heutz, who might suddenly materialize in my sights, a perfect target, paralyzed with stupor. I just had to take one precaution as I entered the grounds: conceal the blue Opel perfectly, preferably in the garage, since that was where the other person had got into the car that had escorted me to Geneva, following me at the very moment when I was going to kill H. de Heutz. Since then, H. de Heutz and his blonde associate must have been looking for me with something resembling rage. They'll come back to their chateau for some peace and quiet eventually, with no idea that it's in their stronghold that I've taken refuge. My strategy can only disconcert them: of its kind it's a small masterpiece. The Prussian blue Opel cabriolet will serve as my Trojan horse to beleaguer the enemy citadel. I, revolutionary agent twice caught off guard, had in a sense disguised myself as H. de Heutz, arrayed in his blue cuirass, outfitted with his false identities, and bearing his heraldic keys. And in that guise I was about to gain admittance to the grand salon where I too will turn my back on the Dents du Midi that were illuminated this morning beyond the big French doors. One thing is certain, my plan is something of a challenge, for according to the current logic of our profession, it could strike one as a rash undertaking par excellence. This illogical appearance, however, is its most formidable quality: it's a counter-disguise! Yes, I'm an innovator. I no longer disguise myself as a tree branch or an innocuous stroller or a bearded tourist weighed down with loaded cameras; my disguise is now that of a victim of the stunning murder I'm about to commit. I take his place behind the wheel of a blue Opel; soon I'll be part of his furniture – indeed, I'm nearly inside his very skin . . .

While I was thus airing my opinion about certain practical concerns pertaining to the murder of H. de Heutz, alias Carl von Ryndt, alias François-Marc de Saugy, the road from Coppet to Rolle was giving me a quick look at the far shore of the lake, a veritable archipelago of rocks and fields of black ice. On the other side, immobile France was running towards the mouth of a river as I drove along at a good clip. As soon as the road cleared a little, I pushed it as hard as I could, making the internal revolutions scream. From Rolle to Aubonne, from Aubonne to Renens, I drove like a sensible adult. Then, shortly after leaving Renens en route to Echandens, I spied across the fields the jagged shape of the chateau, half-hidden by a clump of trees: a dark mass, disproportionate with the little village of Echandens huddled around that enigmatic monster. Discreetly, I parked the car on the shoulder; I even turned off the ignition. To tell the truth, I had the jitters. Suddenly, even before I went on stage, I was uncontrollably agitated. It was dread that was keeping me inside the Opel, even if this was a danger zone where any of the locals could identify the little blue car and would be surprised that its owner wasn't at the wheel. The Trojan horse galloped by night, and I dreamed of realizing the same exploit in daylight under this beautiful sun. Sheer madness! Echandens is small: the whole village would know if a stranger was inside its walls. My scheme bore an odd resemblance to Russian roulette.

I lingered at this spot close to the chateau and even closer to the first houses of the village. An emotion that I couldn't name, unless it was fear, was keeping me there, so close to the danger, in a somnolent state: that, of course, was more a result of the heat and my fatigue than a symptom of my jitters. I stood there, unable to hurry matters, lacking the blinding certainty that urges one to act. I was sinking into debility as into a comfortable bed without putting up the slightest resistance to this generalized bliss. Thus positioned on the outskirts of a battlefield, I ignored everything except my developing numbness and my drift into a fluid and hypnotic respite. I sat there motionless under a roof overheated by the sun, my gaze lost in this elevated plain that could be a slope of the Jura or of the Pre-Alps. I was no longer determined to stay on this road that turns sharply on its way into Echandens; I could fit my spirit to nothing but the paralysis that was gaining on it.

I've stopped moving. To tell the truth, the disturbance no longer affects me: its very impact breaks down into an infinite number of interruptions whose amplitude grows as their frequency increases. Lethargy settles into me solemnly and vigorously in the form of an ecstatic fall. Inside my steel shell I'm as motionless as a Vedic priest; I linger religiously along the way as I approach the stage I'm to appear on. I don't hesitate, rather I feel as if I'm on my last legs, as if I've been injected with a dark cantharis. Nothing more appears on the horizon: neither the Fribourg Alps nor the domes of the Jura nor any hope of getting out of this unscathed. Nothing, not even the surety that in a certain number of days I'll be able to circulate at will, to stroll aimlessly among crowds of people between the windows of Morgan's department store and the stores on Peel Street. No, I don't even know if I'll be able to lounge around for a few hours or days when I'm in the mood, or do nothing and improvise my idleness, choosing my own procedures and place: to hesitate between Café Martin and the Beaver Club, to linger at the bar of the Holiday Inn between a Cutty Sark and the darkly shadowed eyes of the woman I love. Hesitation itself would be a form of movement. But I'm not stirring, I am gliding, motionless, gorged with memories and uncertainties, through poisonous water. Nothing files past now as on the day of our *fête nationale*: my windshield still opens onto the same slice of the Vaudois plateau where a chateau is located that I'm not going to. And between it and me I maintain a distance equal to that separating me from our bedroom on that June 24. This evening it's as hot inside me as in the stifling countryside around

Echandens and on the bed strewn with cushions where we ushered in a tragic season. It's as hot inside me as it was that night when a secret upheaval made the entire town shudder with the convulsions that shook our bodies. Unmoving, I watch my own nothingness pass by; unmoving, I'm like the chateau of Echandens I see now, solid as the snow that buried our first kiss. The reality around and within me is outstripping me: a thousand dazzled crystals stand in for the passing of time. I am stopped in my race. Nothing moves forward except my hypocritical hand across the paper. And from this lingering residuary movement I infer the brain activity that controls it, the embryonic waves that survive imperceptibly during a coma and contradict it since it contains the very principle of its opposite. My cursive handwriting bears witness to a second genesis that, though reduced to zero, is not altogether stopped, simply because my hand doesn't stop racing. And so my torpor is merely a sudden and transient death. From my hand's vibratory course, I deduce that a manic river is discharging into my cephalic vein, its tumult displacing my names, all my childhoods, my failures, and whatever is left of my nights of love. This polluted trickle that gushes onto the page transports me utterly into the confusion of a flight. An uncertain Nile seeking its mouth, this driving current writes to me on the sand along the pages that still separate me from the lugubrious delta. Before me stand unprecedented acts: chateaus, women, hours, centuries. Awaiting me, too, are entire chapters on guerrilla tactics in the heart of Montreal and the record, suicide by suicide, of our unwilling revolution.

Stopped here along a cantonal road in the serene and sunlit countryside, facing my various futures, covered with shame and the past definite but stirred once more, even if only by a wave of unawareness, I decide by unilateral revolutionary decree to put an end to the ataraxia that has kept me pinned to the front seat of the little blue Opel all this time. And if I still can't make out what route to take in the future, except perhaps in the image offered to me by this road as it turns towards the village of Echandens and the chateau, I realize that I just have to start moving again, follow the handwritten curves, and reinvent my story. Indeed there's nothing now to prevent me from having already crossed the village without seeing a soul, parking the car in the garage, going inside the chateau of Echandens and positioning myself at a window in this delightful period prison (since I'm here in any case), after crossing the village without seeing a soul and putting the car in the garage. I've also checked out the property, Mauser in hand, to make sure there was no procurator hidden in one of the chateau's many rooms. It's completely deserted; and during this visit, a hasty one it's true, I've unearthed no mysterious object: no radio transmitter, hidden microphone, or intercom system. On my way down the cut-stone staircase, I took the precaution of opening the inside door that goes from the vestibule to the garage. It's my emergency exit in a way. To escape with a flourish, I can simply go through that narrow doorway, work the handle that lifts the garage door, hop into the little blue Opel, and turn the key I've judiciously left in the ignition.

IT'S STRANGE, being all alone in this grand residence. In every room I race through, I keep discovering *objets d'art*, displayed more or less conspicuously. Just now I'm in the main salon where, this very morning, I had a bad encounter with H. de Heutz. In better shape now to look calmly at what's around me, I admire a two-tiered Louis XIII buffet. It's a remarkable piece: the upper tier, much narrower than the base, opens by means of a single roundel door on which a naked warrior is depicted. Made of amber-coloured wood, its surface decorated with bas-reliefs and friezes seduces me like the skin of an unknown woman. I open the door, which creaks as it moves on its rat-tail hinge. Suddenly another sound is superimposed on the creaking. I stop and listen. If this new sound points to an enemy presence inside the chateau walls, it must be accompanied by other sounds which, added up, would indicate its source, unless my own silent wait is met with either an attempt at silence or an attempt to identify the screeching sound produced when I opened the door of the Louis XIII buffet. Nothing happens. And I quickly attribute my brief auditory hallucination to a perfectly reasonable case of nerves. I go on turning the door: inside the upper tier of the buffet there's absolutely nothing. Strange. I sound the body of the naked warrior: very handsome! I admire his slender form in unstable balance and the majestic way he holds his head. Against whom is he hurling himself like that, brandishing an extravagant lance as his only weapon? Circling the roundel, a carved frieze serves as the warrior's triumphal arch. Two caryatids frame the door so that the upper tier resembles a secular tabernacle set on its altar. There, the solitary warrior is god. Yes, this buffet is truly remarkable. I'm in ecstasy before its closed mass, which stands at the entrance to the salon; I hadn't even seen it this morning because I'd had my back to it so I could face H. de Heutz. I let my fingers brush the smooth bulbs of the caryatids and I caress the carved garments on this empty buffet. Here is where I would truly like to live. The profusion of furniture and *objets d'art*, the entire room now strikes me with all its luminosity. To think that H. de Heutz lives here! His story about children abandoned in Liège is nothing but a secondhand imposture, a kind of monologue drawn at random from the first draft (my own, as it happens), then taken to the limit of improbability in an attempt to make it plausible, for once the man has embarked on his complicated epic, it would be hard to change either plot or character without setting me against him.

How fine it must be to live here, to have access to this big room lit by the valley of the Rhône, to rest here from the hideously overcrowded cities. Life here surely doesn't consist of the same actions repeated wearily, lethargically: it must be altogether different! Here is the big Italian armoire I'd noticed this morning – a masterpiece! The marquetry angels are enchanting: I love them, I really do. Outside, the bright afternoon fills everything with a blinding light that renders the alpine meadow diffuse when I look at it through the thin muslin curtains over the French doors. I sit in an officer's chair, low-slung and very comfortable. From this wide-angle perspective, the salon that so delights me seems even more enticing. It's hard for me not to comply with this interior which encourages one to rest. The fury that drove me from Ouchy to

Château d'Oex, from the Col des Mosses to the Jean-Jacques Rousseau bridge, from the narrow streets of Carouge to this salon and then from Echandens to Geneva and Coppet, seems at the very least inappropriate to this delightful setting I'm studying lazily. I let myself go: it's not dangerous either, because at the slightest click of a lock a few steps will take me to the door in the vestibule that leads to the garage. I fire at H. de Heutz and jump into the car. It's a simple matter of speed and precision and where that's concerned I'm confident.

Yes, I can let myself go a little, as long as I never leave the ground floor. In fact since I checked the two upper floors and concluded with certainty that there's no one in the chateau, I can take up my position in this grand salon with equanimity, staying here with unflagging pleasure. I wait. It's a matter of time. H. de Heutz and the blonde woman who's come to save him must have begun by circling the area around the Baroness de Staël's chateau, certain that I wouldn't get very far on foot. After a few patrols in the area, they've probably broadened their range of surveillance, tirelessly criss-crossing the village of Coppet; at least one of them must have done that while the other was posted at the federal railway station. But before they could even refine their police methods, I had time to cross the woods next to the chateau, rest on the promontory for a few moments, get back on the Grande-Rue and take a seat at a table in the Auberge des Émigrés with an uninterrupted view. Just as H. de Heutz and this woman were carrying out their intensive surveillance of the area around Coppet, I was tucking into crêpes with ham and Emmenthal cheese and sipping my second glass of Réserve du Vidôme. By choosing to stop for a bite to eat at a time so inappropriate for relaxation, I foiled my adversary's plans; I demolished the most erudite theories one can draw up to trap a fugitive who's moving within a restricted circumference. The time I took to enjoy my lunch at the Auberge des Émigrés only mystified them more, so much so in fact that ultimately, to get some peace, H. de Heutz and his woman friend must have accepted the fact that I was nowhere to be found and then, without a word, they've gone back to wait for me in Geneva on Place Simon-Goulart, thinking I'd have to touch down there to get my Volvo back. Wrong! Simon Goulart himself could have been resurrected and the Banque Arabe could have risen up into the air before I went back to that little square encircled by the Alps. As for me, I'm waiting for H. de Heutz, seated in this Louis XV armchair that positions me just above the surface of the lake I can see sparkling in the distance through the cloud of the curtains. H. de Heutz is looking for me, and I'm waiting for him. I have a better chance of meeting him here than he does of spotting me on a bench on Place Simon-Goulart. I relish my position.

The more I look at it, the more I'm enamoured of the lacquered chest of drawers, covered with dalmatics, where a battle is being fought by two soldiers in armour in an explosion of shades of blue and vermilion. On the chest sits a book bound in grainy leather: *History of Julius Caesar: The Civil Wars,* by one Colonel Stoffel, published by Casimir Delavigne, Paris, 1876. I take the precious volume back to my chair, but instead of opening it, I gaze at the magnificent lacquered chest, fascinated by the violent yet peaceful battle adorning this exquisite piece. The two warriors straining towards each other in complementary positions have been immobilized in a kind of cruel embrace, a duel to the death that serves as a luminous veneer for the dark chest. Everything here is astonishing. Every object H. de Heutz has chosen appeals to me. I notice that just above the chest of drawers he's hung a very rare engraved reproduction of "The Death of General Wolfe" by Benjamin West; the original, which belongs to the Marquis of Westminster, hangs in the Grosvenor Gallery. This print is now worth more than the large canvas. It's a genuine masterpiece printed from his original by the painter himself: the few copies include those in Buckingham Palace, the Musée de

Québec, and the collection of Prince Esterhazy. H. de Heutz is one of those unlikely individuals, millionaire or connoisseur, who never makes a mistake. This brilliant copy of "The Death of General Wolfe," which was purchased by George III some centuries before H. de Heutz bought his, thrills me! For that matter the remarkable luxury and good taste throughout this chateau fill me with a kind of haunting memory I've never known before: the pleasure of living in a house can then resemble the bewildered complacency I experience in this sweeping, majestic salon. H. de Heutz lives in a kind of altered universe that's never been available to me, while I carry on my chaotic exile in hotels where I never really live. Through the casement of the French window the exuberant landscape spreads all the way to the misty cliff faces of France across the lake. Ah, how I would love to live in this refuge with all its mellow pleasures, amid the expression of an ancient will to live that has not been lost. A confident power hides behind these well-chosen objects. Draped in its periods and styles, this salon secretly reveals itself to me. Yes, the peeled gilding in the dark texture of Benjamin West's work and the panelling above the parquet floor holds a disturbing riddle. Between Regency and Henri II, in this burst of festooned mouldings and evocations, I try to catalogue the components of a man I've sworn to kill. In vain I attempt to decipher the luminous crypt he lives in, but the beauty of this place fills me with emotion.

Never has H. de Heutz seemed as mysterious as he does right now in this chateau he elegantly haunts. But is the man I'm waiting for the enemy agent I'm to kill in cold blood? It seems unlikely because the man who lives here transcends brilliantly the image of a victim I've composed. This man is defined by something other than his counter-revolutionary mission. His double identity is disproportionate to the role he fills: there's something excessive about his cover, and that worries me. I'm grappling with someone I don't understand. Is the man who purchased that two-tiered buffet, the officer's chair, the chest of drawers with the two warriors, the man who hung Benjamin West's "The Death of General Wolfe" on the salon wall, is he the phony specialist in Scipio Africanus I took aim at near the Château de Coppet? And if it's not H. de Heutz who lives here (or Carl von Ryndt or even the pathetic François-Marc de Saugy, what difference does it make!), who adorns his living space with all these objects, then who is the other person? His partner, his chief perhaps, or the blonde woman – and is she really blonde? – whom I spotted so close to me? How can I know? One thing is certain: K has put me on an absolutely amazing trail. In any event, her instructions have proven to be troubling. Now I'm bursting to tell her about everything that's happened to me since yesterday and describe the unforgettable secret of this chateau deep in the Vaudois countryside. But first I must kill H. de Heutz – cleanly, unhesitatingly – and as soon as the deed is done, take the blue Opel out of the garage, turn right on the road that runs through the village, floor the gas pedal, and make my way to Lausanne, turning left at the Busigny fork.

While I gaze at the lacquered chest of drawers where two tawny-coloured warriors are locked together in death, I leaf mechanically through Colonel Stoffel's book. This artistically bound volume has an anonymous *ex libris* on its flyleaf, something I've never seen except, of course, in stationery stores that sell *ex libris* with a blank space for the owner's name. This one, though, is actually more indecipherable than anonymous. Where the owner's name should be, there's an intricate drawing that coils around itself in a series of loops and whorls that form a Gordian knot, a cluster of initials superimposed in every possible graphic layout. The deeper I plunge into these tangled tentacles that take the place of a stamp, the more I'm struck by the premeditated nature of this masterpiece of confusion. I count an endless quantity of articulations, and as I reconstitute the manifold designs of these lines, I think I can make out some Arabic letters. In this nest of tracery I seem to recognize the scrolls and spiral serifs of the illuminated capitals that start the suras in certain Persian copies of the Koran. Yet as I peer at this hermetic code, I can see that, contrary to appearances, they're not Arabic letters but the initials of the man who's interested in Colonel Stoffel's *History of Julius Caesar: The Civil Wars*. Between this work of military history and H. de Heutz's presentation last night in Geneva on the battle between Caesar and the brave Helvetians at Genaba, there is an undeniable link – just as there's a conclusive correlation between the man who lives in this impossible chateau and the spuriously anonymous *ex libris* in whose depths I'm trying to locate the key to a riddle. This holds true for the entire chateau which mystifies me not so much as a dwelling but as a code. For these engraved chests filled with nothing, these roundels that send back images of war, and this apparently forgotten book that tells of Caesar's battles are just so many initial letters bound together inextricably in a haughty and fascinating knot. It all bears a signature, that of the man for whom I'm waiting.

The bright afternoon flows by in the drowsy countryside. I can make out the muted dazzle in the French doors that let me see in the distance the Alps disintegrating slowly in the bluish water of Lac Léman. Motionless and vigilant, I stand watch here in the enemy camp. Arrayed in the ornamental attributes of H. de Heutz, surrounded by furniture chosen by him, and sitting in his officer's chair close to "The Death of General Wolfe," I've made myself a prisoner of this man, the better to approach him and, ultimately, to kill him.

I wonder in what dark corner the blonde woman who witnessed my conversation with H. de Heutz this morning could be hidden. The grand salon is impractical. The only other place I can imagine is the vestibule that opens on one side onto the main entrance and on the other onto the garage and the spiral staircase that goes upstairs. When I left the salon with H. de Heutz at point-blank range, he was obviously the one who was leading. He'd done nothing more or less than manipulate me as he showed me quite naturally to the front door. And it didn't even cross my mind to question his integrity as a guide, nor did I think of glancing at the other end of the vestibule; but even had I done so furtively, I wouldn't have noticed the woman who, simply by drawing back, could make herself invisible, for example by hiding behind this massive credenza. She could have camouflaged herself easily by standing between the credenza and the frame of the door to the garage. I didn't see anything and I couldn't have seen anything. It's at that very spot in this makeshift sentry box between the immunized piece of furniture and the garage door that I'll position myself presently when H. de Heutz gets here. And if I want to speed things, I just have to keep an eye on the entrance to the grounds by standing behind the door with a peep-hole that opens onto the front of the chateau, allowing one to see any cars that are coming or going. Between there and the credenza there is just the width of the vestibule, that is, two strides. When I see H. de Heutz's car pull up near the entrance to the chateau, I can simply cross the vestibule and stand behind the credenza, ready to open fire on the enemy. Till then I don't have much to do, even though my freedom of movement on the ground floor is curtailed; I'm actually confined to a lookout post that is an isosceles triangle, which I mentally trace by drawing a line between my hiding place and the lacquered chest of drawers with the entwined warriors, another from the chest of drawers to the credenza, and finally another from the credenza back to my hiding place. Inside this Euclidean space then I can move very easily, with no fear of being surprised because from every imaginable position inside the triangle, I can get to my firing position to the right of the credenza in a fraction of a second. I just have to wait calmly for H. de Heutz, while he's probably pacing Place Simon-Goulart, attracting the attention of a policeman on duty, perhaps, or the curiosity of a teller in the Banque

Arabe. Because rashly strolling around outside a bank is liable to lead to a charge of conspiracy.

But I have better things to do than imagine what H. de Heutz is up to in Geneva while I wait in his chateau at Echandens, pacing the front hall and the predetermined zone of the grand salon; especially because picturing my adversary in another town won't really prepare me for his suddenly bursting in. I've deluded myself enough about his machinations up till now. With him you never know. Consequently, I need to convince myself that H. de Heutz is totally unpredictable; then I'll be better able to welcome him appropriately than if I spent my time dreamily, running him through the rather faulty grid of my hunches. I will sense only an infinitesimal part of his power. His epiphanies are disconcerting and they invariably catch me unawares. The impression he makes on me neutralizes my ability to counter-attack. Steeped in improbability, H. de Heutz is surrounded by witchcraft and mystery. The holstered gun on his chest is just a formality: his real strength comes from a secret weapon that in the final analysis may be only a counter-feint. The warrior set into the roundel of the Louis XIII buffet has no armour but his beauty, and presenting himself naked to his enemy may be his greatest strength. The relationship between H. de Heutz and me has left me pensive ever since of my own accord I let myself into this fine lair where he lives.

For the time being I won't allow myself to investigate the two upper floors. Something tells me though that if I were to carry out a scientific search instead of the hasty examination I made when I first came in, I'd come across a whole arsenal of documents, maybe even photos of his wife and his two boys, books on Roman history too, the last shreds of correspondence with unknown women who sign their love letters with just an initial. To tell the truth, though, that's all I would find. As for the evidence of his counter-revolutionary activities, the plausible testimonies of his collusion with the RCMP, and his secret banking activities in Switzerland – those exhibits I certainly wouldn't find. I know H. de Heutz too well. With him, every revealing document is probably encoded with the Villerège grid and a counter-code, so that when the two were combined they'd be totally illegible. I wouldn't find a thing – not the initials of the mounted police or the logo of the CIA or a hint of any records of a bank account where the numerical weapons of our revolution are piling up! On the other hand, it would be pointless, a waste of energy, for me to decode the plan of the Roman fortifications for the battle of Lerida or the inventory of the funerary furniture of the *pontifex maximus*. Such an exhumation of dates and names would get me nowhere and would only add to the nonsensical impression I get from anything having to do with this man.

My watch has stopped at three-fifteen, though I'm sure it's much later, even if I judge only by the fading daylight I see through the French doors. Here I am in the heart of Switzerland without a clock! How can I find out what time it is? It's important because I don't want to miss my appointment on the terrace of the Hôtel d'Angleterre. Bah, I can just pick up the phone in the hall and ask the operator. Then again, maybe I'd better not. You never know. The phone may be connected to a switchboard God knows where. I'd be sounding the alarm to H. de Heutz's command centre. You can never be too careful, especially nowadays when the phone system has become a veritable public square.

I don't know what's going on inside me. Suddenly I'm soaked in sweat. I have an insane urge to explode, to howl at the wolves and to kick at the panelled walls. An unbearable anguish is gripping me: the time that separates me from my sentence is exhausting and infuriating. All my strength pours from my mouth in a haemorrhage of blasphemy and cries. And why must I suffer such upsets in the face of the preposterous void I'm no longer able to confront? I'm a prisoner here! Yet I slipped into this walled splendour of my own accord: I entered here as a masked killer. Now I'm suddenly afraid that I'll never get out, that all the doors are closed forever. My own future is a throbbing pain. I'm haunted not by passive melancholy but by rage, a rage that is mad, absolute, sudden, almost without an object! I want to strike out at random, fire a bullet into the naked warrior, and empty the rest of the cylinder into the lower tier of the Louis XIII buffet. It seems to me that such violence would be soothing: any violence, any shot whatsoever, any feat that would lead to an emotional release! To kill! Kill arbitrarily and without hesitation. I'm beside myself. I feel I'll never be able to leave this place. And while the luminous afternoon is slanting towards the Barre des Écrins, I am confined inside with my funerary furniture. H. de Heutz isn't here yet, but time is passing! Soon – but when, exactly? – it will be time to join K. I have to keep that appointment, for I don't have the strength to face the void that awaits me unless I see K again. Suddenly my whole life is faltering on the big hand of a clock, and I don't even know what time it is! I feel I'll collapse if I'm not within sight of the Hôtel d'Angleterre at half-past six.

Perhaps I'm stuck here for the whole weekend, truly trapped inside an embellished dungeon cell, unable to escape. I can't be! I refuse to go on living and suffering such outbursts of fury. I'm afraid. I come up with a thousand reasons to calm down but they don't comfort me. I'm afraid because I am alone and abandoned. No one comes to me, no one can reach me. Indeed, does anyone even know that I'm in this chateau, armed and with a mandate to kill a man even if I have to wait for him indefinitely? Walls go up around my body, shackles inhibit my movements and grip my heart: I've become a revolutionary doomed to sadness and to the useless explosion of childish rage. My destiny, wrapped in a damask cloth and covered with imaginary furniture, is pitilessly closing in on me. It's horrible to feel destitute in an echoing chateau like this after only a few hours of giddiness, but for how many minutes and centuries yet to come? My strength is gone. And so my entire existence was built on this flimsy base. I'm disintegrating into scattered splinters, shivering at the disastrous passing of time and of my power. I have no resources in this gallery of dreamlike emblems. Nothing ties me any longer to the person who haunts this house. I'm waiting. Ah! I'd sell my soul to know when this waiting will end, to know the precise moment when I can escape from here in a triumphant cloud of dust and get the blue Opel on the road to the Hôtel d'Angleterre. The void that surrounds me seems to emanate from my own shattered existence. The revolution has devoured me. Nothing lives on in me except my expectations and my weariness. Let it come! Let it not leave me alone with myself inside this unfathomable chateau! Yes, let the event fill me once again, let it replace my fatigue ... I want to live thunderstruck, with no respite or a single minute of silence! To bring forth the tumult, to fill myself with war and conspiracy, to be consumed in the endless preparations for a battle: that will be my future!

In this space burdened with memories of H. de Heutz, I am prey to a flood of emotion that fills me with terror and takes me back to childhood. Under the assault of this shadowy discharge I cease to be a man. Ancient tears will pour from my eyes. Three days of seclusion in a totemic motel have not drained all the tears from my body. My failures haven't hardened me. Only the fiery progress of the revolution will beget me anew. Soon, at half-past six, deep in the alpine valley, the revolution will take me to the woman I love. It's the revolution that united us in a gigantic bed above the natal river, then reunited us after a twelve-month separation in a room in the Hôtel d'Angleterre ... Ah, I can't take any more of this dark museum where I'm only hanging on, a warrior naked and perplexed. With a heavy heart I wait for H. de Heutz. The banking memory cracks and melts into the blackness of tears. Finally, the act so eagerly anticipated seems impossible. Violence has broken me before I've had time to commit it. I have no more energy; my own desolation crushes me. I am dying without style, like my brothers at Saint-Eustache. I am a defeated people marching in disorder along the streets that run beneath our bed . . .

How can I grasp the cold wind that is numbing me, how can I name the ill-defined pain that makes me falter? My love, my own! I'm afraid I won't get to the end; I'm weakening. You'll hate me if you learn about my weakness, but here it is all the same, the unavoidable face of my cowardice! I don't have the heart for it. The uncertain revolution is debasing me: I'm not the unworthy one, it's she who is betraying me and abandoning me! Ah, let the event happen, let it generate the chaos that means life to me! Let the event burst, let it give the lie to my cowardice, let it open my eyes! Quickly, for I'm about to succumb to historic fatigue . . . I stay here, with no enemy or reason, far from the violence of the womb, far from the river's dazzling shore. I need H. de Heutz. What will happen to me if he doesn't come? When he's not facing me, in person, I forget that I want to kill him and I no longer feel a blinding need for our endeavour. This interlude in a chateau will get the better of me in the end. The solitary act becomes clouded with the uncheckable progress of this wasted afternoon. No project resists the implacable dimming of expectation. What time is it? I still don't know.

ONE ITEM IS missing from the murderous protocol that will take me back to the terrace of the Hôtel d'Angleterre: the body of H. de Heutz. Without it, I'm stranded in his chateau, which is anguish. Everything has to happen in this space cluttered with furniture, which I continue to explore. The door will open: the click of the lock will be my warning. Without knowing it, H. de Heutz will step onto our battlefield in this narrow zone that separates the place I'll fire from and the threshold of the front door.

And what if H. de Heutz doesn't come back? And what if the revolution never comes to overwhelm our lives? What would become of us then? And what would we have to tell each other at half-past six this evening on the terrace of the Hôtel d'Angleterre?

I wonder if I did the right thing in leaving for the Coppet woods first when I had H. de Heutz in front of me. It would have been wiser to go directly towards the middle of the wooded space. Then he wouldn't have been tempted to escape: one move by him and I'd have fired. And afterwards I'd have been able to flee through the woods as far as the promontory, race down the path that brought me to this little square, then take the Grande-Rue to the Auberge des Émigrés, where I'll have treated myself to an excellent lunch with white wines from Vaud and the Valais; even to celebrate my victory, I'd surely have prolonged the meal with two or three glasses of Williamine from the hills of Hérémence, very near to Evolène and the Valais chalet I dream of buying one day as a place to shelter our love. Clearly I was wrong to run away at the appearance of the blonde woman coming to the aid of H. de Heutz, who followed me throughout my journey from Echandens to Geneva and from Place Simon-Goulart to this small road that turns sharply after the Coppet chateau. There's no doubt about it: I lost the initiative at that moment and that was when the time I'd gained earlier began to turn against me. The coordinates of the plot are tangled. I've dropped the thread of my story, and here I am in the middle of a chapter I don't know how to finish.

Outside, the season is waning. In just one afternoon the whole summer is leaving, turning majestically towards the west. The sadness of the departing season mingles with my equivocation and weakens me. It's not just the summer months that are racing towards the Grandes-Jorasses, but my own youth and our story that began one spring on the road from Acton Vale to Richmond, on our way to that secret rendezvous, when the declining sunlight brushed with a tragic glow the last vestiges of the snow that had fallen gently, when you and I fell into the first bed where we loved each other. The story of our country's revolution is entangled with our desperate embraces and our nights of love. The first sparks of the FLQ united our lives. Together everywhere, naked but secretly united with our brothers in the revolution and in silence, it was amid the odour of gunpowder that we learned the exalted movements of the pleasures of the flesh and the terminal cry. A vast rifle range, our country's snow-covered soil recounts our love to us. The impure names of our cities repeat the boundless conquest I learned once again when I conquered you, my love, with my imperfect, frenzied caresses and the games of death. Your native land gave birth to me, the revolutionary: upon your lyrical expanse I lie down and live. Deep in the darkness of your belly I strike, fainting with joy, and I find the warm and wounded land of our national invention. My love, you are my native soil I scoop up by the handful, dark elusive soil I make fertile, where I fight to the death, prideful inventor of an endless guerrilla war. On this Eastern Townships road between Acton Vale and Richmond, near Durham-sud and wherever we two have travelled – to Saint-Zotique-de-Kotska, to Les Éboulements, to Rimouski, to Sherbrooke, to La Malbaie for three days and three nights, to Saint-Eustache and Saint-Denis – never have we ceased preparing for the war of our liberation, joining our liberated intimacy to the terrible secret of our shattered nation, uniting armed violence with the violence of the hours we've spent loving each other. Entwined, dazzled, in a tormented country, we've tumbled, united inside a single kiss, from one end to the other of our snowy bed. From town to town we've sought not escape, but the absolute brotherhood of the revolution. Nor was it solitude that fed our passion, but the notion of a river of brothers marching nearby and preparing awkwardly for battle. The sound of their footsteps hammered at our passion and their sorrow made our bodies swell. While my fingers were creasing your dress, we listened to their manifold breathing. Our love, unfurling, traces the black calendar of the revolution that I'm anticipating madly, that I'm calling by your name! Our love is preparing for an insurrection, our nights of kisses and delirium are so many dazzling stages in the events to come. Even as we succumb to the spasm of the night, our brothers are struck down by the same sacrilegious event that joins our bodies in a lyrical synthesis.

WHILE THE SUN is slanting towards my deadline and the light in the valley is dwindling, I'm exhausted in the midst of the empty furniture and silence. I feel care-worn, almost inclined to petulance, for I'm far from the rolling countryside of Durham-sud and the twists and turns of the Saint-François River. I'm an exile from the Nation and my life. I travel through the vast museum of my clandestine existence, far from the declaration of independence of Lower Canada and of the fertile plain that stretches between Saint-Charles and Saint-Ours, far, too far from highway 22 where we drove by night in the driving rain. From where I am I do not hear the bouzoukis on Prince Arthur Street or the West Indian band from Pointe-Claire. Nor do I see the snow that still falls on our childhood, in the same way that it shrouds eternally the Aiguilles Rouges and the dark Dents du Midi.

The duel to the death between two lacquer warriors has suddenly taken on the tawny shade of fear. The surface they cover is strewn with funereal highlights. Ferragus's double lives here. This artfully engraved furniture, these caskets carved or covered with marquetry, and "The Death of General Wolfe," all suggest the fearsome identity of the master of the premises. The man who lives in the tomblike splendour of this home, who knows the code of the *ex libris* in the *History of*

Caesar and the riddle in which I wrap myself – that man gets away from me time and again. The author of this cryptogram of false meetings and ambiguities is looking for me even harder than I've been pursuing him. A murky obsession draws me into its transience. While he seeks me out, I slip my weapon inside his armour: I uncover his bare flank and his smooth warrior's skin. It is his very skin I touch with my feverish fingers when I brush the Genoese velvet that clothes the indecent texture of his real presence, revealed to me by the veiled surface of the naked warrior. According to some new measurements, our encounter, so often avoided, is making progress. The more he eludes me, the more I approach him. And if the plain on which we're moving seems to grow bigger between the Arve and the Sarine, the site for our next meeting is concentrated between the Henri II credenza and the Dutch door, a veritable battlefield lined on the south by the big Italian armoire and the lacquer chest of drawers, and on the north by the picture rail that runs along the vestibule from the front door to the dropped ceiling at the open door that leads to the garage through which I'll leave. Since last night I've been pursuing H. de Heutz. I finally feel that I'm about to face him again. I stay here in his officer's chair at the very centre of his existence; secretly I've become part of him, joining myself indistinctly to the warriors who cover his furniture and to General Wolfe who is dying across from the city of Quebec.

He's here! The muffled humming of a car, the crunch of gravel in the entrance – it's him! From my surveillance point behind the peep-hole, I can make out the rear end of a grey car with a Zurich plate. In fact, I've arrived too late to see the car drive onto the chateau grounds, but never mind. This is not the time to start questioning everything. I swing into action; I cross the vestibule to get back to my point of attack. I squeeze the butt of the revolver in my belt. And now I am leaning against the cold wall of the chateau, my shoulder level with a bunch of grapes carved in high relief on the credenza which hides me completely. Soon H. de Heutz will open the Dutch door. On my right I see the garage door that will give me instant access to the instrument of my escape. The time has come. No sound yet to indicate that H. de Heutz is at the porch. I hear absolutely nothing, and I'm not indifferent to that. I should have put my ear against the keyhole: then I could have heard what was going on outside; perhaps I'd have even been able to tilt the upper half of the door to hear clearly the premonitory sounds of the enemy bursting into the range of my weapon. But I've stopped moving. My fingertips are icy from the frantic throbbing of blood in my temples. Not a single movement or sound, not even that of my own breathing. All is silence. Expectation keeps me shuddering and upright. Very slowly I take the 45 from its improvised holster. Moving precisely, I bring it up to my chest, the barrel pointed at the antique wooden grapes. I release the safety and now I just have to wait a few more seconds. I have no intention of trying to stay hidden to fire at H. de Heutz, for my position behind the credenza doesn't guarantee effectiveness. I'll spring from my hiding place and take advantage of his surprise to solidify my attack position, steadying my armed hand with my outstretched left fist held perfectly parallel to my shooting arm. Ultimately, I'll have to concentrate on my aim, think of nothing but my target, and not worry about fending off a counter-strike that H. de Heutz won't have time for.

But what can he be doing now? He's had more than enough time to get from the grey car to the door but I've heard nothing. It's too late to cross the vestibule again and take a look outside. If he were to catch me, I'd be thrown off balance, having lost the few fractions of a second that secure my advantage and without which I'd be much less certain that my aim was accurate. I have no second choice, ever since I've delimited this battlefield after analyzing the structure of the space. What time is it? All at once the air moves! He's inside, but he hasn't closed the door. He takes two steps. He still hasn't shut the door; maybe he's waiting for the other person. But why is he stopping? The crystalline ring of the telephone reassures me. Nothing has happened between us yet. As long as he's on the phone, H. de Heutz won't budge. If the other person doesn't answer, I'll make my move.

"Hello, is that you, my love? I've just arrived. It's been an unbelievable day . . . You can't imagine; I'll tell you all about it later. What about you, any news? . . . You think I can trust him? . . . No, I've never seen him, I'm sure I haven't. You know, I'd like to meet you and finalize this whole business, do you understand? . . . This evening then, soon: the time it will take me to get there. Let's say half-past six on the terrace of the Hôtel d'Angleterre . . . But I absolutely have to see you: it's urgent. I'm sure you can put off the other one or deal with it in a few minutes . . . Look: I'll take a table near the orchestra, in any case he doesn't know me. When you're finished with him, you can join me . . . You have to understand. I can't take any more, my love. This whole business is turning out very badly for me. I'm afraid; yes, I fear the worst . . . I absolutely have to see you later on . . . Look: above all, don't forget the colour of the paper and the code, do you understand? You'll find it in Stoffel's account of the battle of Uxellodunum on page 218 . . . Now tell me: where are the children?"

THEN, NOTHING. The voice deepens in my memory while the wind from the Vaud blows in my hair and I wander alone around the Château d'Ouchy. Under the dark water of the lake, my near east is flowing towards the Montreal Prison. I linger on the enchanted shore. I look at the tiered streets of Lausanne that we covered from top to bottom one night, strolling from Place de la Riponne to the Quai d'Ouchy, down the paved rue des Escaliers-du-Marché that winds its way along one of the dried-up arms of the Thièle. The city is all lit up now; the other night its lights were doused in the augural dawn that poured from our bed. The Château d'Echandens is obliterated in the dark water as I stroll for the thousandth time along the terrace of the Hôtel d'Angleterre. Little happened between my departure from H. de Heutz's chateau and my arrival on the terrace of the Hôtel d'Angleterre, but late for my meeting with K. She'd gone. Now it is growing dark; an orchestra at the end of the terrace attacks the first chords of "Desafinado." Groups of passersby stand on the sidewalk listening. I should add that the terrace is full to overflowing with customers. Once again I go up to some tables and look at all the faces, but they tell me nothing. K isn't there, but I go back all the same, you never know, she might return. "Desafinado" makes me face up to the cruel facts: I've lost my

106

love! And I don't even know how to retrace her in Switzerland: perhaps she was due to leave tonight for Berne or Zurich. How can I reach her? I don't know her cover or that of her office. I stand there in a daze, staring sadly at this carefree crowd and all the lovers whose knees brush under the tables: *they* have been able to find one another. There are a good many. I can't help but see a wonderful beauty in them, merely because they're together, whereas I've come here too late to meet the woman I held in my arms yesterday, as day was dawning behind the closed shutters that look out on the orchestra and the whole valley of the Rhône. Yes, it was in the room I'm gazing at now that we loved each other. And it was marvellous! K, naked and warm and lying beside me . . . Truly, we were beautiful, joined together, reunited at last after so many misunderstandings and wasted months. I've loved other women in the past, I've thought I loved them, but all my memories have merged in K's blazing belly.

I stand near the terrace, my back to the Savoyard Alps that are displaced in the shadows, and I know that I've lost the woman I love. I have lived to meet her and I'm now dying pointlessly of love. Where are you, my love? Why did we separate after the incandescent dawn that burst from our embrace? Why, on the shore of the deferred lake, did we reinvent this revolution that broke us and then reunited us, that seems impossible to me this evening while I stand watch in this haunted crowd and the orchestra plays "Desafinado"? The underground revolution is breaking us once again in the depths of our exile here on the terrace of the Hôtel d'Angleterre that I love and where I live to infinity, like the poet who died at Missolonghi. You are so beautiful, my love, truly more beautiful than any of the women I stare at now, methodically. Your beauty bursts with power and joy. Your naked body tells me again that I was born for real life and that when I love, I desire frantically. Your blonde hair is like the dark river that flows at my back and surrounds me. I love you the way you appeared to me the other night when I was walking towards Place de la Riponne, complete and invincible, and I love you when you're tumultuous, when you cry out our pleasure. I love you draped in black or scarlet, dressed in saffron, veiled in white, clad in words and transfigured by the dark shock of our two bodies. The wind from the Vaud that delicately tangles your blonde hair brings me the perfume of your flesh, but where are you? Does this secret wind come from the lake or from the hot plain of Echandens I've just come from, but too late? Ah, now that I've lost you, I'm delirious. I feel that I'm brushing against your damp flesh, that I'm drunk with your secret odour. I remember a long-distance call I made from the Lord Simcoe in Toronto, and in this funereal room where I'm a prisoner of nausea and terror, I feel threatened once again. Something has broken: the interruption has just occurred and I don't know how to talk to you. I want to tell you: come, follow me, we'll live together, but I have forty-eight dollars in my wallet, not even enough to buy you a one-way plane ticket to Toronto. Events overcome us, shattering me into a thousand pieces. I'm stammering in this bed at the Lord Simcoe. Toronto is sinking into Adriatic amnesia. You slip away and no one told me that one day in Lausanne . . . How many months will pass before I'm with you again, my love? To what city that I don't yet know will the uncertain future exile us? The next time – but after how much renewed anguish, how many wasted nights? – perhaps I'll meet you on Rashid Avenue in Babylon, or in the land of dear Hamidou (whom I've lost track of) in the Dakar medina, or under mosquito netting in the Hotel N'Gor; in Algiers perhaps, or in Carthage near Bourguiba's presidential palace . . . Or perhaps I shall never meet you again.

I stand motionless in the midst of this wild crowd that awaits our dazzling appearance at the window of our room. But you're not here . . . This evening I begin my life without you. Ever since I've known that I've lost you, I've been aging at a terrifying speed. My youth has taken flight with you: centuries and centuries are carved into my inert body. People are looking at me, no doubt because of the sudden erosion that's stamped on my face, and maybe too because I'm crying. Our story is ending in me badly. It's dark. Everything dies if I've lost you, my love. I walk through this happy crowd that exasperates me. It's not you who abandoned me, it's life. Surely it's not you, is it? One can't see anything on the lake: the absolute night shelters me and settles in between us irrevocably.

I am walking in this foreign country, a man who has just lost you after finding you again by chance, joyfully, on a street in Lausanne and in a romantic bed at the Hôtel d'Angleterre. In the distance I hear the chords of "Desafinado" as I move away from the terrace of the Angleterre without even turning around. I no longer have a country, I've been forgotten. The torn Alps whose dark crenellations I can glimpse across the lake no longer bewitch me. The things we loved together have no meaning any more, not even life. Even the war, alas, since I've lost contact with your sovereign flesh, you, my only country! Starting now, I am living a glacial night. I own nothing except a gun that's become ridiculous and some memories that are rendering me harmless. Where are you, my love? Trees swollen with darkness stand around the Château d'Ouchy and along the wharf where we two strolled at nightfall. That was last night. In the distance I can make out the confused sound of discordant music and a laughing crowd. I did not kill H. de Heutz. In fact I wonder what overwhelming coincidence made him want to go to the terrace of the Hôtel d'Angleterre at half-past six, to meet a woman – the blonde, perhaps? – he talked to on the phone. But he'll never keep that appointment. Unless he turns up late, like me. Because if I've lodged a bullet in his shoulder, he may have found a way to have it tended to, then get into the grey car with the Zurich plates and, driving with one hand, arrive in Ouchy. Perhaps at this very moment he's pulling up at the noisy terrace I've just left.

That speculation disturbs me. I retrace my steps. If he's there, I want to see him, but even more I want to see the unknown blonde woman he arranged to meet on the phone just before our exchange of gunfire. I quicken my pace. No doubt I'm returning in vain because the blonde woman got tired of waiting for H. de Heutz. She has gone. And so H. de Heutz too will be alone and won't know what to do. The terrace is as lively as ever; passersby stop to listen to music that has no meaning for me. I go back to the Hôtel d'Angleterre once again with the unfounded hope of finding K, who may have come back to the terrace too in desperation, hoping my absence was merely a delay. Lovers stroll nonchalantly, arm in arm, along the lakeshore, projecting their own emotion onto the unfathomable landscape that fills me with desolation. I'm here on the sidewalk, on the same side as the hotels that look out on the lake. I go up to the terrace of the Hôtel d'Angleterre, my heart pounding. I push aside the people who block my view. I look at all the faces. I scrutinize the back of the terrace. Just next to the orchestra I spy a blonde head. Who is it? Her face is hidden. She's talking to a man, but he's not H. de Heutz. I scan the overpopulated quadrilateral: every blonde woman attracts my attention, but none of them is you! It's as if Lausanne only gives birth to blondes. I've never seen so many. But clearly, K isn't here. I hope in vain; I die a thousand deaths whenever I spot a blonde head. Ah, I've always lived as I am living at this moment – at the outer limit of the intolerable ... Tonight, all these blonde heads cause me pain because you're not there and I'm looking for you desperately. I realize that it's a waste of time: there's no sign whatsoever of my earlier life on the enchanted terrace of this hotel. It's as if I'd never come here with K, as if I'm surrendering to a fine hallucination, and the Hôtel d'Angleterre exists only in my devastated brain, like the Vaudois chateau where I spent my life waiting for a certain banker who's interested in Caesar's African wars and who abandoned his two sons in Liège so that he could rob all the banks in Switzerland! I rave in silence, surrounded by the din of this terrace crowded with people observing me as if I were an intruder. I decide to go to the hotel office. It's hard to navigate through the tables, I keep stumbling and bumping into people.

The desk clerk recognizes me right away and favours me with a big grin.

"Here, Monsieur (and he remembers my name), there's a message. The lady asked me to give it to you; she said you'd be dropping by."

The clerk holds out a sealed blue envelope with no address.

"If you'd like a room for tonight, I can offer you one with a view of the lake, the same one you had yesterday. It's free again."

"No, thank you . . ."

"Goodbye, Monsieur . . ."

With trembling hands I open the blue envelope while I'm still in the lobby. I recognize K's beautiful handwriting and I read her latest message: "The boss had an unexpected visitor this afternoon. Something incredible, I'll tell you about it later. Bank transactions suddenly disrupted. I leave for the north tonight; the boss is going to visit friends on the Côte d'Azur. No matter how your approach to the bank president works out, I imagine you'll go back to Montreal to see to our interests there. Come back. K." As a postscript, she has added two lines: "Hamidou D. sends his regards. It's a small world . . ."

VERY LITTLE time passed between my solitary stroll along the shore of Lac Léman and my arrest in Montreal in the middle of summer. After I read K's message, everything came in a rush in disorderly succession: my departure from Lausanne, the firing of the four Rolls-Royce engines of the Swissair DC-8, the flight that looped over the range of the Jura, the endless celestial nothingness and then passing through federal customs at the Dorval airport. All things considered, nothing happened between my departure and my forced landing, nothing except the time it takes to move from one city to another in a high-speed jet. In Montreal I first went to 267 Sherbrooke Street West. There I found several open-necked Hathaway shirts, some books scattered here and there, and a keen sense that I had come home. Meanwhile, K was somewhere in the Hanseatic mist of Antwerp or Bremen, not with me; I'd become once more a lonely man deprived of love. I checked the newspapers; I found nothing about our "interests." From a phone booth I tried to reach my contact: the operator (recorded) told me repeatedly that the number I had called was not in service. Very well. Now what? Thinking it over, to readjust more quickly, I walked endlessly. Of course I could risk proceeding irregularly since I couldn't reach my contact by phone. Why not take the risk? After all, I'd have to establish a relationship with a member of the network. I decided to speak to M by phone. Just then I was ambling along Pine Avenue past the Mayfair Hospital: I went down the Drummond Street staircase, then stopped at the Piccadilly for a King's Ransom. After that I made my way to the phone booths across from the Québecair office in the hotel lobby and dialled M's number. We exchanged some remarks that would be disconcerting to the RCMP wiretappers but were meaningful to us: through this hypercoded language I learned that our network had been short-circuited by the anti-terrorist squad, that several agents had been detained in the Montreal Prison for nearly three weeks now, and that, as might have been expected, the money collected by our tax specialists was now part of the central government's consolidated budget. A disaster, in conclusion, which M had miraculously escaped. Upset by these ambiguous revelations, I downed another King's Ransom at the Piccadilly bar. The next day I cleared out my savings account at the Toronto-Dominion Bank, 500 Saint-Jacques Street West. I pocketed a hundred and twenty-three dollars in all, enough to live on for eight days, with no luxuries. From the outside phone booth across from Nesbitt Thompson, I called M again as arranged. We agreed to meet on the stroke of noon in the lateral nave of Notre-Dame basilica near the tomb of Jean-Jacques Ollier; of course we didn't mention the illustrious abbé's name or utter that of the old church whose presbytery stands next to the Montreal Stock Exchange.

It was precisely eleven when I stepped out of the glass booth. And as I had an hour to kill, I strolled down rue Saint-François-Xavier to Craig Street and went into Mendelson's. I love that place; when I go inside, I always have a hunch that I'm going to turn up General Colborne's pocket watch or the revolver with which Papineau would have been well advised to kill himself. On my left as I came in was the collection of swords and sabres, including a Turkish scimitar I'd have liked to hang above my bed. But I knew from experience that their knives are generally overpriced; for that matter, I know the clerk and he's intractable: no bargains to be got from him. I went to look at their helmets; I was particularly struck by a Henri II armet, a dilapidated object with a very impressive curve. They were asking forty dollars; I could have bargained a little and got it for less. It still would be an extravagance though, in view of what I had in my pocket. Besides, what would I do with this helmet? Next to it there was a full set of armour: gauntlet, couter and armband. It was sixteenth century, rather hard to identify but a fantastic model. The disjointed arms in black iron had something tragic about them and resembled a hero's amputated limb. If it were on the wall of the apartment, I'd be unable to look at it without shuddering. To escape the clerk's enthusiasm, I went back to the front of the store where a showcase held an amazing number of pocket watches and other timepieces. I've always been fascinated by old pocket watches: I like their two-part gold cases covered with arabesques and the engraved initials of their former owners. I looked at a few just to kill some time. Finally, I noticed a pocket watch, its gold dull but elegantly engraved with the monogram of some anonymous dead man. My mind was made up: I took out a ten-dollar bill. But the clerk reminded me that I'd have to add the cost of the chain, making twelve dollars and seventy-five cents in all. Oh well, it wasn't exorbitant; and I really did want a pocket watch to measure lost time. The case, made in England, contained a Swiss movement which turned with eternal steadiness. I moved the hands to the correct time: precisely eleven-forty-five. My time had come.

I went back onto Craig Street, then climbed the steep hill up Saint-Urbain in the direction of Place d'Armes and crossed it diagonally. Before I entered the church, I bought a newspaper. As usual, I was careful to retrace my steps, zigzagging a little to thwart anyone who might be following me. I entered the Aldred building at 707, then left at once through the door on Notre-Dame. I ran across the street, and after a few athletic strides I was inside the dark church.

There was something terrifying about the silence inside: suddenly the mystery of this dark enchanting forest grabbed me by the throat. My footsteps rang out all around. I went to the transept, spotting no one in this deserted church and hearing nothing but the multiplied echo of my own procession. A shuddering purity filled this sacred place. I was a few seconds ahead of M, and while I waited, I sat very close to the secondary apse, lost in contemplation and prayer. I was careful not to open my newspaper in an excess of enthusiasm, though I longed to see if there was anything about the preliminary investigations. When M showed up, coming towards me from the altar (God knows how!), I repressed a surge of emotion. Everything happened so quickly. There was a sound on my right: the door of a confessional opened. I caught sight of a properly dressed man who came hurrying towards me. Then another individual seemed to loom out of the transept crossing. He too was respectable looking. M and I had time to exchange a desperate look but not a single word. They led us to the porch. We went out by way of the staircase on rue Saint-Sulpice, our wrists shackled. An unmarked car was waiting; we piled into the back, following the police orders. I know the rest: an informal event that had gone on not being fulfilled for three months' time, an uninterrupted series of stains and humiliations that take me into the death-like density of writing.

I am alone, a prisoner in solitary, sneakily transferred to a nearly forgotten institution. Time has fled and it continues to move away while I am sinking here in a plasma of words. I'm awaiting a trial from which I can expect nothing and a revolution that will restore everything to me . . . Ah, I can't wait to run again in the unoccupied vastness of my country, to see you in the flesh, my love, in another way than seeing you disappear into the frail opacity of the paper. Where are you? In Lausanne or in your apartment on Tottenham Court Road?

The endless period of my imprisonment is my undoing. How can I believe in the possibility of escape? A thousand times I've tried to get out: there's nothing to be done. One link is still missing from the sequence of my escape. Actually, a logical conclusion will always be absent from this book. Armed violence is missing from my life and so is our boundless triumph. And I long to add this final chapter to my private history. I'm stifling here in the counter-grid of neurosis while I cover myself with ink and, through the impermeable glass, brush against your legs that keep me prisoner. My damp memories haunt me. Once again I'm walking on the Ouchy wharf between the ghost chateau and the Hôtel d'Angleterre. Failure comes back to me as forcefully as unfinished deeds and inert shreds of the tattered Alps. When I burst out of the Château d'Echandens, I'd already ruined everything.

". . . I'll take a table near the orchestra, anyway he doesn't know me. You can join me when you're done with him . . . You have to understand. I can't take any more, my love. This whole business is turning out very badly for me. I'm afraid; yes, I fear the worst . . . I absolutely have to see you later on . . ."

The formulas stop in her mouth and fill me with a wave of vague fear. Everything is snarled; the time I can recall is fleeing. Movements are disjointed. As I prepare to leap, I wait endlessly for the proper moment, my finger on the trigger. From one moment to the next, surely I'll find the word I need to fire at H. de Heutz. All is movement, yet I'm frozen here, waiting just a few seconds before I strike on target.

". . . I'm afraid; yes, I fear the worst . . . I absolutely have to see you later on . . . Listen: above all, don't forget the colour of the paper and the code, do you understand? You'll find it in Stoffel's account of the battle of Uxellodunum on page 218 ... Now tell me: where are the children?"

At these words, I moved. And rather than continue all the way, I broke my synergetic thrust: something in me gave out, but H. de Heutz became aware of my presence. Two bullets grazed the mouldings on the Henri II credenza, even before I'd recovered enough for a counter-attack. The intermittent gunfire that went on then broke the sacred ritual of my *mise-en-scène*: our battle was fought in the most shameful disorder. I'm positive I hit H. de Heutz with at least one bullet; but I'll never know for certain if I killed him. In fact, I'm quite sure I didn't; indeed, I don't even know exactly where I wounded him because I dashed to the garage door without turning around. That was when I heard another shot. He probably collapsed to the floor when he was hit and it was from that position that he tried desperately to shoot me. Or had he crouched behind a piece of furniture to protect himself, using that ruse to force me into being discovered? One thing is certain, I drove through the chateau grounds at the wheel of the blue Opel in a spirited finale without even protecting my rear. After failing at everything I wanted to do except my flight, I found myself after a hectic race on the terrace of the Hôtel d'Angleterre. That was when I realized that not only had I missed H. de Heutz, but by missing him narrowly, I had just missed my appointment and failed at my entire life.

K had gone again and I had no way to contact her. In a quandary because she wasn't there, I was broken, desperate in a way one's not allowed to be when one sets out to make a revolution. For a long time I prowled around the terrace of the Hôtel d'Angleterre, feeling that I'd spoiled everything. At best, I had wounded H. de Heutz in the shoulder – but at what a price! Here I am, undone as a people, more useless than any of my brothers: I am this wreck of a man who is wandering aimlessly on the shores of Lac Léman. I stretch out on the Abraham page and lie on my stomach to die in the blood of words . . . I'm trying to find a logical ending for everything that's happened, but I can't! I long to be done with it and to place a full stop on my indefinite past.

THE BLONDE woman who was hovering around H. de Heutz is pursuing me like a nightmare. I haven't seen her head-on; at no time have I been able to look at her, so it would be impossible for me to identify her today. Her power over me is as uncertain as it is boundless: I'll never be able to recognize her. She is totally unknown to me, and if I start imagining (but this doesn't hold up!) that the man I tried to kill in a lordly chateau in the Canton of Vaud is not H. de Heutz, I'll never know how wrong I was or why that man treated me as an enemy. No, this assumption leads me to the perfectly unknowable, for I'm no longer in a position to authenticate H. de Heutz . . .

If K were with me, if we had met on the terrace at half-past six as agreed, if I'd given her a description of the inconceivable man I'd pierced with a bullet – near the heart, I hope! – she would confirm that the individual is indeed the enemy triple agent who could single-handedly make all our banking operations in Switzerland fall through. One thing is certain: K would tell me that it was indeed H. de Heutz whom I'd spent too long waiting for in Echandens. And now I am rotting inside four walls that remind me of neither H. de Heutz's chateau in the Vaud nor the room where we lived passionately in the Hôtel d'Angleterre.

If I hadn't exhausted my strength waiting for H. de Heutz, I would have killed him with precision, and once I was back in Lausanne, I'd have offered K a job; I'd have asked her to put me in touch with Pierre, the head of her organization, leading to a profitable union between our two networks. I'd have explained my position clearly to Pierre (whom I've never met, as it happens); and there's no doubt that we'd have come to an agreement about tactics. With his consent, I'd have been in a position to work continually in liaison with K, meaning in Lausanne or Geneva or Karlsruhe, everywhere! We'd have made love at dawn in hotel rooms Byron occupied before he volunteered for the national revolution of Greece . . .

My tardiness for our meeting was a disaster: from that moment on, my life was shattered. When I came back, all I found was the enigmatic message the desk clerk handed me with the discouraging smile of a bailiff holding out a subpoena. It's strange: I didn't even wonder if the blue note was some enemy machination whose only purpose was to hasten my return to Montreal and consequently my capture in a church. At no time did I question the authenticity of the message, and I don't remember bothering to identify K's handwriting, so overcome was I. Anyway, who else could have left a sealed message for me at the front desk of the Hôtel d'Angleterre? No one knew that we were supposed to meet on the terrace at half-past six. Absolutely no one. The reference to Hamidou, of course, makes me wonder: K knew him, but how could she know that I knew him too? And then . . . rather than grow disheartened as I am now, I'd prefer to postpone the analysis of a series of events whose causal logic I lack the power to reconstitute just now. I'll see it all clearly later on when I'm reunited with the woman I love. In the meantime, I have no right to question myself about anything because by doing so I continue to obey H. de Heutz, who throughout this business has used every imaginable means to make me doubt. I sense that whenever I give in to disenchantment, I am obeying him and making myself conform with the diabolical plan he's woven against me.

But this is not the last word. In any event I must keep myself invulnerable to doubt and stand firm in the name of what is sacred, for within me I carry the germ of revolution. I am its impure tabernacle. I am an ark of the covenant and of despair, alas, for I have lost everything! I feel that I myself am finished; but everything inside me is not. My story is interrupted because I don't know the first word of the next episode. But all will be resolved and end on a high note. I trust blindly, even though I know nothing about the next chapter, absolutely nothing, only that it's waiting for me and will sweep me away in a whirlwind. All the words of the sequel will grab me by the throat; the ancient serenity of our language will be shattered by the shock of my story. Yes, the unchanging nature of the subject of my account will suffer the impious terror; revolutionary letters will be painted by rifles all down the length of pages. Since Cuba's July 26, I have been dying in sterilized sheets while the foothills of the Alps surrounding our kisses fade away in me a little more every day. One certainty comes to me, though, of what's to come. Already I have a premonition of the unbearable tremors of the next episode. I tremble at what I haven't written. Unsure of everything, at least I know that when I finally rise up against this incomplete régime and from my prison bed, I won't have enough time left to lose my way again in my story, or to link the series of events into a logical structure. Already it will be very late, and I won't waste my energy waiting for the propitious moment or the favourable instant. Then it will be time to fire at point-blank range – in the back if possible. The time to kill will have arrived, as well as that – an even more pressing deadline – for organizing the destruction according to the ancient doctrines of discord and the canons of nameless guerrilla warfare! Parliamentary struggles must be replaced by warfare to the death. After two centuries of agony, we'll make dissolute violence burst out, an unbroken series of attacks and shock waves, spelling out in black a project of total love . . .

No, I won't finish this unpublished book: the final chapter is missing and I won't even have time to write it when the events occur. When that day comes, I won't have to make up the minutes of lost time. The pages will write themselves in gunshots: the words will whistle above our heads, the sentences will shatter in the air . . .

When the battles are done, the revolution will continue to unfold; only then perhaps will I find the time to bring this book to a final stop and to kill H. de Heutz once and for all. The event will occur as I predicted. H. de Heutz will go back to the funereal chateau where I lost my youth. But this time I'll be well prepared for his reappearance. I'll watch and wait for him. When the iron-grey 300SL with Zurich plates makes its appearance, it will strike me as obvious, it will send me into action. First, I'll tiptoe across the distance between daylight and the Henri II credenza while I trip the safety on the revolver. And as soon as I feel the bolt move in the lock, H. de Heutz will come on stage and, unbeknownst to him, move into my range. I'll shoot him before he even gets to the telephone; he'll die blinded by the knowledge that he has been trapped. I shall bend over his body to see the precise time on his watch and, as I do so, I'll realize I have time to get from Echandens to Ouchy. And that's how I shall arrive at my conclusion. Yes, I'll emerge victorious from my intrigue, calmly killing H. de Heutz to rush to you, my love, and close my tale in grand style. Everything will end in the secret splendour of your belly, populated by slippery Alps and eternal snow. Yes, that is the conclusion to the story: because everything has an end, I shall go to meet the woman who's still waiting for me on the terrace of the Hôtel d'Angleterre. That's what I'll say in the final sentence of my novel. And, a few lines later, I shall write in capital letters the words:

THE END

Afterword

BY JEAN-LOUIS MAJOR

Shortly after two o'clock in the afternoon of March 15, 1977, Hubert Aquin was found lying on the road beside his car, a red 1976 two-door Ford Granada, in the park surrounding Villa Maria, a private school in the middle-class neighbourhood of Notre-Dame-de-Grâce near his home in western Montreal. He had shot himself in the head. Blood and brain tissue were splattered as far as the large elm trees standing more than twenty-five feet away, but his dark-blue suit with matching light-blue shirt, silk vest, and tie remained undisturbed and immaculate. He was forty-seven years old.

Neither the manner nor the circumstances of Aquin's death, nor even, for that matter, the fact of his death, has anything to do with the novel you have just read or anything else he ever wrote, except those few short letters he left unmailed and unstamped as was his habit, advising friends of his previously and elaborately discussed decision to commit suicide. The manner and circumstances of his death, however, have much to do with Hubert Aquin as literary icon, and thus with the manner in which everything he wrote is now regarded and, sometimes, read.

When he committed suicide, Aquin became the exemplary literary figure for the post–Quiet Revolution and post–Parti Québécois–election period. He thus replaced Paul-Émile

Borduas, the intellectual godfather of the Quiet Revolution, who had lost his job as a teacher at the École du Meuble in 1948 for writing *Refus global*, a pamphlet of incendiary rhetoric, and died in Paris in 1960 at the age of fifty-five.

Conditions for admission to the pantheon of martyrs of Quebec literature are not clearly defined: membership varies according to prevailing ideological currents. Conservative moods have long favoured Octave Crémazie, the nineteenth-century poet who died in exile in France to avoid going to prison after his Quebec City bookstore went into bankruptcy. Liberal times attribute a more exalted status to Louis-Antoine Dessaulles, the fiery journalist and anticlerical polemicist who, in 1875, had to follow the same route as Crémazie after resorting to a number of falsifications to avoid bankruptcy. According to others, this group should include essayist and novelist François Hertel, who moved to France in 1949 after leaving the Jesuit order, but it now seems Hertel has been eclipsed by poet, novelist, and literary critic Louis Dantin, another former cleric, who fled to Boston, where he became a typographer at Harvard University Press at the beginning of the twentieth century.

For some time in the forties and fifties, and even well into the sixties, Hector de Saint-Denys Garneau seemed to meet all the requirements to be considered a literary martyr. He published a single collection of poems in 1937, and died at the age of thirty-one in 1943, after living in seclusion in the family *manoir* since the age of twenty-two. Despite having published so little, Saint-Denys Garneau's image suffered from the fact that he had died of a heart attack, notwithstanding the efforts of some of his admirers to present his death as a suicide or, even better, a collective murder. On the other hand, poet, playwright, and cosignatory of *Refus global* Claude Gauvreau, who was long associated with Paul-Émile Borduas and in fact became the self-proclaimed leader of the Automatist movement when Borduas left Montreal for New York and, later,

Paris, seems to meet all the essential conditions for membership: he committed suicide in 1971 after having been interned in various mental institutions. In Gauvreau's case, the difficulty arises from the fact that he wrote abundantly, if somewhat obscurely.

The paradigm for these mythic figures remains the poet Émile Nelligan, who, at the age of eighteen, was locked up in an insane asylum where he remained for forty-two years, without ever writing another line of verse, until his death in 1941. In the 1980s, Nelligan was the subject of a biography that was at least ten times the size of his collected poems; he was even the subject of an opera written by playwright Michel Tremblay and composer André Gagnon. Nelligan's poems may have gone out of print, but his biography is now available in paperback.

That is more or less the company Hubert Aquin joined in the collective imagination immediately upon his death. What is exceptional about Aquin's situation is that he had already attained an equivalent status upon publishing his first novel, *Prochain épisode*, in 1965. That he became a mythic figure at such an early date is due to a unique convergence of circumstances, social, political, and personal, as well as literary. This latter aspect, however, would normally be the least of considerations: one of the advantages of literary martyrdom is to give non-readers the opportunity of knowing all there is to know about a writer without having to change their own privileged status.

Although *Next Episode* is set in Switzerland, this story of a Québécois terrorist on a mission to murder a counter-revolutionary whose identity and role remain problematic is imagined and narrated by a terrorist who was arrested and sent to a psychiatric institution before he had the opportunity of setting out on his own destructive mission. The narrator's predicament in the novel mirrored that of Aquin himself at the time he wrote *Next Episode*: he was being held at Institut Albert-Prévost after being arrested for driving a stolen car and carrying an illegal firearm. Upon being arrested and asked his occupation, Aquin had stated that he was a revolutionary. In less felicitous circumstances, he would later publish an essay titled "Profession: Writer."

At the time of his arrest, Aquin was well known as a producer and director of radio and television programs for Radio-Canada and documentaries for the National Film Board. He had also been a member of the editorial board and, for a few years, the editor of the literary magazine *Liberté*. Aquin was thus closely associated with the institutions that defined and nurtured Quebec's literary elite.

Though a brilliant intellectual who wrote some of the most illuminating essays in Quebec literature, Aquin remained somewhat of an outsider. His novels were highly acclaimed in Quebec, but rather than the traditional image of the writer, he more closely resembled, at least outwardly, the stockbroker that he was for a while, or even the banker or businessman that he aspired to be – he was the founder and president of a company that tried to organize Grand Prix racing in Montreal – if not the race-car driver he dreamed of becoming.

Through all that, how was *Prochain épisode* read? Aquin is an author on whom an exceptional number of monographs, theses, and articles have been written – though not as many as on Nelligan, naturally. The question remains, however: Was Aquin's novel really read? And if so, how?

If you are reading this afterword, it probably means you have resisted the lure of mythology and have ventured into reading the novel, unless you are cheating. But how did you read the novel?

I remember my own sense of amazement the first time I read this novel. I was immediately fascinated by the power and beauty of the opening sentences. With its internal echoes and intriguing, contradictory images, the first sentence will forever be imprinted in my mind: "*Cuba coule en flammes au*

milieu du lac Léman pendant que je descends au fond des choses
(Cuba is sinking in flames in the middle of Lac Léman while
I descend to the bottom of things)."

The resounding images, altogether visual, intellectual, historical, and deeply personal, which flow from the opening
metaphor, set the tone for a flamboyant narrative alternating
between reflective chases and vertiginous immobility. But is
it a quest for hope, a narrative of defeat and despair, or an
affirmation of collective will and a blueprint for revolutionary action?

No interpretation excludes all others, but I have difficulty
understanding how this novel could be read otherwise than
as a modern fable of Romantic despair. Unless, of course, its
meaning is presumed to follow from the purported revolutionary intentions of the author.

Everything in *Next Episode* is set in counterpoint and
inverted images. The narrator imagines dashing figures of
revolution and counter-revolution in vivid contrast to his
own desperate situation. Yet the characters he creates are
strangely ineffective and constantly shackled by doubt and
ambiguity; they flounder about, without a clear purpose, in
a world that is painfully beautiful and where nothing is truly
what it seems.

"I am the fragmented symbol of Quebec's revolution, its
fractured reflection and its suicidal incarnation," writes the
narrator of *Next Episode*. The inescapable paradox of the
novel, however, arises from the fact that collective identity is
a source of depression and, ultimately, of defeat and despair,
rather than the foundation for revolutionary action. Because
it is dictated by the collective disability, the novel itself
becomes a form of suicide: "I give in to the vertiginous act of
writing my memoirs and I start writing up the precise and
meticulous proceedings of an unending suicide." Thus, the
writing of the novel, however accomplished, does not generate a form of liberation; rather, it is a measure of defeat.